A MILLION REASONS

WOULD YOU KILL FOR A MILLION DOLLARS?

MARK DAVID ABBOTT

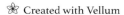

For G
She thinks I'm awesome.

JOIN MY VIP NEWSLETTER

The next book is currently being written, but if you sign up for my VIP newsletter I will let you know as soon as the next book is released.

By signing up for the newsletter you will also receive a complimentary copy of **Vengeance,** the first book in the John Hayes series, as well as advance notice of all new-releases.

Your email will be kept 100% private and you can unsub-scribe at any time.

If you are interested, please visit my website:

www.markdavidabbott.com
(No Spam. Ever.)

1

MACAU

Player Eight wiped his sweating hands on the legs of his trousers as he watched the attractive young lady deal four cards from the shoe, two which she slid face down in front of him, and two she tucked under the corner of the shoe. She waited, her face expressionless, as he reached for the cards and slid them closer. He took a deep breath and carefully peeled up the corner of the first card to see what fate had dealt him. He needed a good hand —surely his luck would turn. He saw the red heart first, then the number. A two. So far okay. He tossed it onto the purple felt of the table and slid the second card closer. Positioning it lengthways, he peeled up the side, shielding the card from view with his cupped hands. *Pook Kai,* Shit. An eight. In the rules of Baccarat, a total of ten meant zero as the first digit was dropped. He threw the card on the table for all to see and with a shaking hand reached for the glass of cognac on the table beside him. His right eye twitched as he brought it to his mouth and downed the contents in one large swallow. The dealer slid the Banker's cards out from under the shoe, and one by one, turned them face up. A King and a three —

thirteen, but as the ten is dropped, the Bank's score was three. He exhaled loudly and reached for his glass again. Realizing it was empty, he waved the glass at the hostess and glanced at the two hard-looking men in ill-fitting black suits, standing on the other side of the red velvet rope separating the VIP enclosure from the rest of the gaming hall. They made little attempt to disguise their interest in him. He would have to worry about them later. Now, he had to focus. He nodded at the dealer, and she slid another card in front of him. He wiggled his fingers, then peeled up the side of the card. *Tiu leh lo mo!* Motherfucker! A queen. Another zero! The dealer drew another card for the Bank. Again ten, but she was still ahead with three. Another loss for him. Shit! What did he have to do to get Lady Luck on his side again? He was sitting at position eight, his lucky number, and in his pocket, he had the jade beads his grandmother had given him years ago for protection, but still, he was suffering. At seat number five, an obese, middle-aged man from mainland China chortled with unbridled glee, his bet on the winning Banker's hand resulting in a large payout. He pulled his winnings closer, his stubby fingers festooned with gold rings, and added them to the already large pile in front of him. Next to him at number three—there being no number four on the tables in Macau, the number inauspicious as it sounded like the word for death—sat an older, casually dressed man, his slightly accented Cantonese suggesting he was a Macau local. He had also lost the hand but looked relaxed, his expression giving nothing away— neither happy nor unhappy about the result.

Player Eight's fresh glass of cognac arrived, and he leaned back in his chair and took a large swig while deciding what to do next. Despite the arctic-like temperature in the VIP section, beads of perspiration dotted his forehead. He had been playing all night... or was it now morning? He had no idea, the passage of time cleverly hidden from the gamblers by the Casino, and he had already pawned his Rolex.

The evening had started well, and he had been up for the first few hours. In retrospect, he should have quit while he was ahead, but he couldn't leave the table, the allure of the cards having immense power over him... and he had been on a winning streak, intending to make back all his previous losses and be in profit. He had to ride the wave while Lady Luck was with him. He had played on and on, the pile of chips growing higher in front of him... Then in one cruel moment, Lady Luck abandoned him and didn't return. He had lost hand after hand, the pile of chips in front of him dwindling as the hours passed. After the previous hand, he was down to his last hundred thousand. He really should get up and leave the table for a while. Wait for his luck to change...... but then he would have to deal with the thugs in suits outside the rope. No, he would play one more hand, all or nothing. He slid the remaining two chips into the square marked Player. The dealer looked at the mainlander who selected two gold chips from the pile in front of him and also placed them on the Player square. Player Eight bit his lip. Two million dollars! If only his luck had stayed with him, he would have some gold colored chips too. Both players looked over toward the Macanese man and waited for him to bet. His fingers played a gentle rhythm on the table felt, then he slid a chip into the Banker's square. Attention now turned toward the dealer who again dealt four cards, slipping two under the shoe and sliding two across to the mainlander who, as the player who had placed the largest bet, had the honor of revealing the cards. He grabbed them with his fat fingers and without waiting, turned them over and tossed them on the table. A ten and an eight, a "natural" eight, the second highest hand in Baccarat. He shouted something in Mandarin and with his fist, pounded the table in delight. Player Eight breathed a sigh of relief. Finally. There was no way the Banker's hand would be higher. It was merely a formality now. The dealer turned over the first card. A ten. The mainlander laughed while the Macanese player looked on, a slight frown the only indication of his mood. Player Eight took another large mouthful of Cognac, gulping it down as he waited for the dealer to reveal the final card. She looked around the table, pausing for suspense, then flipped the card over. Player Eight's mouth dropped open. A nine, the only hand that could beat them. He was finished. He loosened his shirt collar and reached for the glass, his hand shaking so violently, he almost spilled the drink on the table felt. He gulped it down, the fire of the drink bringing tears to his eyes. Pushing back his chair, he rose unsteadily from the table.

The other players looked up at him, the Macanese player with sympathy—he had been there before, but the mainlander, despite his own loss, sniggered and said something in Mandarin that sounded derogatory. Player Eight wasn't sure, he couldn't hear anything, his head was pounding, and he felt dizzy. He turned and stumbled toward the exit, the security guard unclipping the velvet rope to let him pass. As he stepped out, the two hard men in suits closed in on him, grabbing him by the arms. One leaned in and whispered in his ear, "Broken Tooth wants to see you." His knees trembled, and but for the men holding his arms, he would have collapsed on the floor.

2

The courier van indicated and slowed, causing one of Hong Kong's ubiquitous red and white taxis to honk in frustration. The van pulled to a stop, and a man dressed in a courier uniform opened the passenger door and jumped out. Jogging around to the back of the van, he held his hand up in front of the taxi, holding up the traffic as the van pulled forward, then reversed into the empty parking space at the side of the street. The courier stepped to the side and waved the taxi on, the taxi driver cursing him through the open window before driving off.

A young man in chinos and a polo shirt finished paying for a bottle of water in the 7-Eleven across the street and turned to look out through the store's open front. He watched as the driver climbed out of the van and joined his colleague at the back. They unlatched the rear doors and started sorting through the packages stacked inside.

The young man pulled out his phone and pressed speed dial.

"Standby."

On the next street, a white Mercedes Sprinter van sat, engine idling, orange hazard lights blinking in warning. The driver removed his earbud from his right ear and turned to the van's darkened interior.

"Get ready."

The courier van driver pulled out a large package from the rear of his vehicle and scanned the bar code with a hand-held scanner. He straightened up and glanced toward the 7-Eleven. Catching the eye of the young man, he gave a slight nod, then walked toward the entrance of a nondescript apartment building that loomed high over the street. His colleague closed the van doors and stepped onto the pavement, looking both ways before following the driver to the entrance.

In the 7-Eleven, the young man brought his phone to his ear again. "Five minutes."

The courier walked into the grimy entrance lobby while his colleague took up station outside on the pavement. In the lobby, the elderly security guard looked up from behind his desk and seeing the courier's uniform, simply nodded and went back to studying the racing form in his newspaper.

The courier summoned the lift, and when it arrived, he pressed the button for the tenth floor. The ancient lift creaked and groaned as it climbed higher, the courier sweating in the confined space. He looked for a switch to turn on the fan, but the tiny fan was insufficient to cool the narrow steel box. Sweat formed on his upper lip, and his shirt began to stick to his back. At the tenth floor, the lift shuddered to a stop, the floor of the lift not quite stopping at the same level as the corridor floor. The courier took a deep breath and as the doors opened, exhaled slowly. He stepped out and checking the address on the parcel, matched it with the sign on the wall and turned right to find the correct apartment. He stopped outside a steel grill and pressed the dirty switch that functioned as a doorbell.

He waited and after a minute, heard the sound of bolts being slid back, then the door creaked open just enough for the person inside to peer out.

"Courier," he called out.

From inside, a face looked him up and down. Satisfied he was who he said he was, the door opened wider, and a hand reached out to unlock the grill. The courier pulled it open wide and stepped forward, holding out the package.

Inside, a gaunt middle-aged man nodded and reached for the parcel, the skin on his bony arm almost translucent. He was shirtless, his ribs visible through his parchment-like skin, and he looked much older than his years. The courier held out the scanner and indicated the man should sign with his finger on the screen. The man placed the parcel on the floor, sniffed, and wiped his nose with the back of his hand before taking the scanner from the courier and scrawling his name in Chinese characters across the screen. The courier looked down at the screen, smiled and looked up at the man. "*N-goi sai*, thank you." He turned and walked back to the lift as the steel grill closed behind him.

Once out on the street he looked again toward the 7-Eleven and nodded. Inside the 7-Eleven, the young man raised his phone to his ear once more.

"He's there. Go, go, go!"

I nspector Jimmy Leung of the Hong Kong Customs Drug Investigation Bureau crossed the road, stepping between a taxi and a chauffeur-driven Mercedes. He glanced down at the Mercedes number plate, 888, and grinned—a very auspicious number. Hopefully, it was a sign. He needed some luck. The last few raids they had carried out had been too late, their targets tipped off, clearing out well before Jimmy and his team arrived. He trusted his team with his life, but somehow, from somewhere in the Bureau, the information was leaking out. Jimmy stepped onto the sidewalk and nodded at the two men in courier uniforms who were deep in conversation with the driver of the Mercedes Sprinter.

"Well done, guys," he said as they snapped to attention. He waved at the traffic building up in the street, partially blocked by the double-parked van. "See if you can get this traffic moving again."

The building lobby was cordoned off, and one of his men was questioning the unhappy-looking security guard. Jimmy rode the lift to the tenth floor, stepped out, looked around for the correct apartment, and strode in. Sergeant Anson Wong, the leader of the team that had raided the apartment, grinned back at him.

"Success, sir. Ten liters of GBL, three kilos of Ice, two kilos of Ecstasy and cannabis buds, and around three hundred thousand in cash. I would say about one point seven million in street value, sir."

"Excellent, well done." Jimmy breathed a sigh of relief. Finally, the long hours and hard work were paying off. He glanced at the thin, shirtless man sitting in the corner, watched over by one of his men.

"Have you got much out of him?"

Anson removed his baseball cap emblazoned with the Bureau's initials and ran his fingers through his hair. He sighed and shook his head.

"He's not saying anything. You know how they are with their code of silence."

Jimmy pursed his lips and nodded slowly. "Take him away and lock him up. He looks like a junkie himself. Let's see how silent he is once he doesn't get his regular fix."

Jimmy turned and surveyed his men. "Well done team. It's a good result. Let's get this place cleaned up."

3

"I love you Charlotte."

"Do you think I don't know that, Mr. Hayes?" she giggled, her blue eyes catching the sunlight and twinkling with mischief.

John grinned and reached out to brush the curl of blonde hair from her forehead. He looked down at her lips, inviting him to press his against hers, and he leaned forward. Before their lips touched, Charlotte frowned.

"John?"

"What's the matter?"

She pulled away as the sunlight disappeared and the sky darkened.

"John, help me."

"Charlotte, what's the matter?"

Her face dissolved into nothing, replaced by the face of a man in his twenties, four days' growth of beard on a fleshy, weak jaw, his dark eyes set deep in their sockets, and his lip curled in a sneer. John felt his breath on his face, hot and rank, a mixture of stale cigarettes and liquor.

"Charlotte," cried John, his heart pounding. "Where are you?"

In the darkness surrounding the man's face, three more faces appeared, each regarding him with contempt. He called out again, "Charlotte." The men laughed, and he tried pushing them away, his fingers finding nothing but empty space. Finally, from somewhere in the distance, her voice, "John, help me...."

John woke with a start, his heart racing and his t-shirt and the sheets damp with sweat. The luminous hands on his watch on the bedside table showed five-thirty. He exhaled and laid his head back on the pillow, waiting for his heartbeat to slow again. The last nightmare had been over a month ago, and he had hoped they had finally stopped. John sighed, swung his legs over the edge of the bed and sat up. He switched on the bedside lamp and rubbed his face. The silver-framed photo on the bedside table caught his eye, and he picked it up. He missed her dearly.

Charlotte had been the only woman he ever loved, and not a day went by when he didn't think of her. He touched his fingers to his lips, then the photo before setting the frame down. There was no point in trying to get back to sleep now. Barefoot, he padded across the cool marble floor into the bathroom. He flicked on the light and ran the cold tap, splashing water on his face, rinsing off the sweat, and slicking his hair back. Leaning with both hands on the vanity unit, he regarded himself in the mirror.

The beginning of yet another monotonous week—five days of soul-destroying boredom in a job he hated. Where had it all gone wrong? Just two-and-a-half years ago, his life had been wonderful—a beautiful wife, an interesting and challenging job, the future rosy. His hands gripped the edge of the basin, the knuckles turning white as anger welled up inside him. He took a deep breath, then exhaled slowly. He didn't want to go there right now.

Straightening up, he turned off the tap and returned to the bedroom to change into the running gear he had laid out the night before. Once dressed, he walked out into the living room, just large enough for a two-seater sofa and a TV, and into the even tinier kitchen. He poured himself a glass of water and gulped it down before retrieving his running shoes from the hallway outside his flat. He laced them up, then slipped his door key under the doormat, and caught the lift down to the ground floor, walking out onto the entrance podium of his apartment building. Despite the early hour, the air was already warm and thick with humidity. John still hadn't got used to it.

He loosened up his head and shoulders and glanced across at a couple of elderly Chinese practicing Tai Chi. He nodded a greeting as he watched them move with a gracefulness that belied their advanced years. John had tried it when he first moved to Hong Kong but needed something more physical, something to get the adrenaline going and boost his mood. He craved the endorphins that only came from hard, physical exercise, and Tai Chi just didn't cut it. He continued his cursory warm-up and light stretches, then headed onto the road for his run.

The first few minutes were always uncomfortable—it took John a couple of kilometers to warm up, to start enjoying the run. From his apartment building, he headed downhill, past the school toward the beach before looping back around Headland Drive, past the multi-million dollar houses he could only ever dream of affording. His mind wandered as he ran, thinking of the day ahead, and he stepped up his pace as a sense of dread threatened to consume him.

At this early hour, there were a few other runners on the road, all trying vainly to avoid Hong Kong's notorious heat and humidity. Apart from a few months in winter, you could never really escape it. John's shirt was already soaked through with sweat. The route wasn't a long one, about five kilometers, but without the run, he was a mess. It made him feel good, the endorphins giving him the boost that enabled him to deal with the day ahead. He pushed himself faster for the final kilometer, gaining satisfaction from passing another runner before slowing just before his building. Drenched in sweat and his heart pounding, he felt strong, confident, and ready, the memories of his bad dream replaced with a sensation of pleasant exhaustion.

John had been in Hong Kong for almost eighteen months, and he loved the city. It was filled with an indefinable buzz and energy which he had experienced nowhere else. His time in India had accustomed him to crowds, but he had never got used to the chaos of an Indian city. Here in Hong Kong, things were different. It was crowded, the city never slept, but the city was efficient and safe, and that's what he needed. It was his job he despised. The yawning chasm of loneliness that threatened to envelop him whenever he remembered his previous life didn't help either.

After the dreadful incident in India, he hadn't been able to settle. He couldn't return to work in the same company, and the faces of the men he had killed haunted his nights. He was drinking too much, not sleeping enough, and lonely. Terribly, terribly lonely. He'd needed a change, needed to pull himself out of a rut, so he bought a one-way ticket to Hong Kong, far away from all the people he had known before, far away from everything that reminded him of his beautiful Charlotte. He wanted to start afresh and heard the city was exciting and that plenty of jobs were available in his field of banking. Exciting it was, the energy tangible as soon as he stepped off the plane, but finding a job was much harder than he thought. He couldn't speak Cantonese or Mandarin, and the international banks were increasingly localizing their staff and cutting costs with less and less of the bloated expatriate packages that had previously been the norm.

Eventually, two months after arriving, he found a job working in a small financial advisory firm—the word adviser a misnomer. John was essentially a glorified salesman, flogging insurance products and funds to people who didn't need them. But he needed the work. The city was expensive, and his funds had almost run out. He had nothing left from his previous life, having sold and disposed of everything.

He was still in a rut, only the location had changed. It was only sheer willpower and his morning runs that helped him face the day.

4

It was over an hour with the air-conditioning turned on full before John had cooled down enough to have a shower and dress for work. He used the time to do some breathing exercises he had learned in India, followed by a few minutes of seated meditation, sitting on the cool marble apartment floor. The meditation was supposed to help him deal with the trauma of the past, but he wasn't sure if it was helping. He did relish though the few minutes of stillness and persisted in the practice, hoping eventually, his flashbacks would end. By the time he finished, a pool of sweat surrounded him. He mopped it up with a hand towel before making a pot of coffee and heading for the shower prior to getting dressed.

Despite the tropical climate, he was still expected to wear a suit and tie for work, no doubt a colonial hangover from when the British ruled over the island nation. It was completely impractical, but old habits seemed to die hard. Consequently, John would always wait until the last minute to get dressed—he hated arriving in the office sweating despite having taken a shower. Showered and changed, he glanced at his watch, realizing he had to leave immediately if he was going to catch his ferry. Straightening his tie, he picked up his wallet and phone from the bedside table and paused to look at the photo of Charlotte.

His eyes filled with tears and a lump formed in his throat as he gazed at the beautiful woman in the photo. She was brutally taken from him during their time together in India, and the memory of what happened still cut through him like a knife. Her killers got away with it because of their connections and a corrupt and inefficient system, but he had wanted retribution. So, he hunted them down himself, killing them one by one, avenging her death, giving her the justice she deserved. It hadn't brought her back though, and any satisfaction he had felt in his revenge had soon worn off, replaced with a hollow pit of despair. He had hoped the change of scene would help him, but he was just going through the motions, filling the days with meaningless tasks. He didn't think he was depressed, he just lacked all motivation. If it wasn't for his runs in the morning, he would probably have descended into alcoholism—or worse.

John blew a kiss at the photo. "I miss you, Charlie," he whispered, then turned and headed for the door.

John lived on Hong Kong's largest island, Lantau and had a choice of commuting by train or ferry. He often took the ferry as it was the highlight of his work day, the journey taking him across the harbor, through the small islands, and past the anchored container ships towering like multi-story buildings above the ferry before reaching Hong Kong island with its spectacular skyline and the verdant jungle-clad slopes of Victoria Peak. He never tired of the view, the sight of thousands of skyscrapers emerging out of the ground like stalagmites, each building swarming with people striving for success like hives filled with worker bees.

The ferry docked in the shade of the International Finance Centre, and John disembarked with his fellow commuters, heading along the overhead walkway connecting the ferry terminal with the IFC Mall, joining thousands of fellow wage slaves heading to their gulags. John weaved among them as they shuffled along, staring at their phone screens, cut-off from the world around them. Not for the first time, John wondered at the futility of it all, spending every waking moment doing something you didn't enjoy in the hope of a few years of freedom when you retired.

He exited the IFC and crossed over Des Voeux Road, following the overhead walkway through the Central Market building and onto the Central to Mid-Levels escalator, the longest outdoor covered escalator system in the world. At eight hundred meters in length and with an elevation of over one hundred and forty meters from its start in Central to its end in the ritzy district of Mid-Levels, it transported thousands of pedestrians every day up and down from the Central business district to the expensive apartment buildings in Mid-Levels.

It was still too early for the escalator to move in the upward direction. Until ten in the morning, it moved downward, bringing executives to their offices. So, John climbed the steps next to it for two blocks before descending to street level. He needed another coffee before work and had a favorite place to buy it.

John pushed open the door of the small cafe and smiled at the young Nepalese man behind the counter.

"Good morning, Thapa."

"Good morning, John. Your usual?"

"As always," John smiled. He came here every morning. The coffee was good, and over time, he had become friendly with the young Nepalese owner. John watched as Thapa weighed out a portion of coffee beans and poured them into a small grinder on the rear counter. Thapa stood about five feet ten inches, tall by Nepalese standards and moved with the grace of a big cat. He turned toward the coffee machine and smiled at John, the corners of his eyes crinkling up.

"How was your weekend?" he asked.

"Not long enough as usual."

"I know what you mean. I only took Sunday off, and I'm feeling tired today."

"Nothing a few cups of coffee won't fix, right?"

Thapa laughed as he prepared the coffee.

John had been coming to Thapa's little coffee shop since he had started his job at the financial firm, and their daily greetings had gradually developed into a friendship. Sometimes, John would escape the office on the pretense of seeing a client and would come down and have a chat over coffee with Thapa who was always friendly with a ready smile. Thapa didn't speak much about himself, but John had pieced together his story during their many conversations.

Thapa was the son of a Gurkha, the ferocious Nepalese fighting force that had served the British Army for over two hundred years. His father had been stationed in Hong Kong for ten years, patrolling the border with China when Thapa was born. Like many other Gurkhas, Thapa's father stayed on in Hong Kong after leaving the army and settled in the bustling district of Yau Ma Tei in Kowloon. Thapa went to a local school and became fluent in Cantonese while his father established his own security firm, providing employment for the retired Gurkhas and their offspring. Times had been tough, to begin with, his father struggling to compete with the large established firms, his mother having to work as a domestic helper. Money had always been tight, and his parents had never been around, working long hours to pay the rent and put food on the table.

Left to his own devices, Thapa had fallen prey to the triad recruiters who hung around the playgrounds and housing estates, looking for disaffected youth and promising them status and fortune among their ranks. He got involved in petty crime, thefts, bullying, and minor extortion. Nothing major but he was headed for more serious things when one of his uncles took him under his wing and explained to him what would happen to him if he continued. He took the place of his absent father and taught him about the great and honorable history of the Gurkhas and how as the son of a Gurkha, it was his responsibility to uphold their reputation even though he wasn't serving in the army.

Something struck a chord, and from that moment, Thapa changed and knuckled down at school, devoting time to his studies, striving to make his father proud. He graduated from high school and not wanting to pursue higher education or become a security guard with his father, he went into business for himself. With the help of relatives, he scraped together enough money to start his coffee shop, and in a tribute to his heritage, the sign above the shop held a very special logo—two crossed Khukuris, the curved fighting blades always carried into battle by the Gurkhas.

"Just how you like it." Thapa handed over John's black coffee in a takeaway cup. "Are you coming in later?"

"Thanks, Thapa. I'll see how it goes. Have a great day." John took his coffee, nodded at the next guy in the queue and walked out the door, turning right, up the hill toward his office on Lyndhurst Terrace. The firm occupied the top floor of a building with multiple tenants. He rode the lift, then tapped in the security code on the keypad at the office entrance. The double glass doors opened directly into the reception area and a large counter, behind which sat two receptionists. He wished them good morning, and they both ignored him. To the left of the reception was a glass-walled conference room with expansive views of the office towers of the Central District, and behind the conference room, a short corridor led to the open plan space that housed John's desk and those of his ten other colleagues.

Most of the desks were already occupied, but no-one was working. Some were hunched over their desks, eating breakfast from polystyrene takeaway containers while others browsed the internet—not a single person acknowledged John as he walked in. At the rear of the open space was the manager's office, the desk facing inward where he could watch over the staff despite the stunning view from the floor to ceiling glass windows behind the desk.

John sat down, took a sip of his coffee and switched on his computer screen. He sighed and rubbed his face with his hands—eight hours of mind-numbing boredom stretched ahead of him. He again thought back to his time in India and his job where he had been in charge of a team numbering almost forty. A team of intelligent and eager young Indians, excited to build their careers and make a difference in the world. Now, he sat under the ever-watchful eye of a boss who did little himself while John replied to hundreds of meaningless emails and made phone calls to people, trying to sell them financial products they didn't need. John shook his head and took another large swig of his coffee, willing the caffeine to kick in before his environment and thoughts of the day ahead pulled him deeper into a depressive funk.

Putting off his actual work, he opened his browser and

scanned the headlines on a couple of news sites before logging into his bank account to check how much money he had left until payday. His salary never seemed to last the whole month. He typed in the password and checked his card balance. The credit card was nearing its limit again, no surprises there. Switching windows he looked at the current account balance. What the...?

That can't be right! He blinked rapidly, looked away, then looked back again. No way! John glanced over his shoulder to make sure his colleagues weren't looking, but he needn't have bothered. They were all in their own private worlds, playing online games or trawling social media. He looked back at the screen, his heart jumping. There was something wrong. Where the balance should have read only a few hundred dollars, there was a much bigger number...

One million dollars!

ohn minimized the screen and stood up, his heart pounding in his ears, and his palms were clammy. He walked out of the office toward the reception desk and grabbed the toilet key from the reception counter before heading down one flight of stairs to the shared men's toilet. Unlocking the door, he walked inside, pulled the door shut behind him, and locked it.

For the second time that day, he turned on the tap and splashed cold water on his face. Leaning on the sink bench, he stared into the mirror as water dripped off his nose into the sink below. One million dollars! Where the hell did that come from? It wasn't his, that much was obvious. Obviously, a banking error, but what was he supposed to do with it? Could he keep it? He certainly needed the money. One million Hong Kong dollars wasn't a fortune—not quite one hundred and thirty thousand U.S dollars—but it could get him out of the rut he was in. He could clear his credit card debt, quit this dead-end job, start fresh, travel... But what if he spent the money and the bank asked for it back? Would he get thrown in prison? Shit.

He straightened up and turned around. He wanted to walk around, to help him think, but there was no space in the toilet. Taking a deep breath, he wiped his face with a paper towel before walking back into the office. He sat down in front of his screen, and after looking over his shoulder to ensure no one was watching, opened the browser window again. A warning message popped up, saying he had been inactive for too long, did he want to continue? He clicked on 'continue,' and the screen brightened up as his bank account filled the screen. It was still there—one million dollars. He scrolled down to the transaction history to establish where the money had come from—deposited the previous Saturday in twenty deposits of fifty thousand dollars, in different branches around Hong Kong. That's weird. There was no clue who had deposited the money. Each transaction simply read 'Cash Deposit.' Who the fuck deposits fifty thousand in cash? And why so many deposits? Who has that amount of cash?

John heard one of his colleagues moving around behind him, so he quickly logged out and stared at the blank screen, thoughts racing through his head like hamsters on speed. What should he do, what should he do? The money would change his life, but he couldn't keep it. It wasn't right. He wasn't a big believer in Karma—he made his own—but he didn't want to tempt fate. Making a decision, he looked at his watch. The banks were open. He picked up his cell phone from the desk, pushed back his chair, and walked out of the office.

"I'll be back in ten minutes," he told the nearest receptionist who didn't bother to look up from the bowl of noodles she was slurping. John shook his head, pushed the door open, and walked into the lobby to catch the lift down to the street. Once on the street, he looked left and right, deciding where to go. He chose right and headed down toward Hong Kong's infamous bar area, Lan Kwai Fong, deserted and decidedly seedy-looking at that time of the morning. In the street, an elderly street sweeper swept up broken glass and discarded beer cans with a bamboo-handled broom while an old lady, her spine twisted and bent at right angles, flattened cardboard boxes and stacked them on a handcart. John found a quiet space in the doorway of one of the shuttered bars and pulled out his phone, scrolling through his phone book until he found the number for the bank.

He waited while it rang, then was greeted by a female voice in Cantonese. Ignoring the Cantonese, John switched to English.

"Hello, I have an inquiry about my account."

The bank employee switched languages, "Good morning Sir. How can I help you today?"

John sighed and started again. "There seems to be an error with my account balance. There is a deposit in my account that shouldn't be there."

"Okay, sir, first I will need to verify a few details. How can I address you?"

"My name is John Hayes," he replied, then answered the rest of her questions—his date of birth, Hong Kong ID number, and mailing address.

"Please wait, sir, while I check your account."

He stood and waited as a delivery truck rolled slowly past before stopping outside one of the bars. The driver and his co-driver jumped out, both stripped to the waist, a sheen of sweat glistening over the brightly colored tattoos that covered their backs. John watched as they unloaded crates of Carlsberg and New Zealand wine onto the footpath.

John loosened his tie with his left hand and tapped his

foot as he waited. His shirt stuck to his back and a bead of sweat trickled down his forehead.

The girl's voice came back on the line. "Okay, I see your account now. How can I help you?"

"Well, someone has deposited one million dollars into my account in deposits of fifty thousand. It's not my money, and I don't know where it has come from."

"But Mr. John, the records show cash deposits. Are you sure you haven't forgotten? A payment for something? Or maybe some friends have put it there?"

"I don't have many friends, and those I have don't have any money. There is no way I would forget a deposit of that amount."

"What do you want me to do, Mr. John?"

"Well, can you find out where the money came from and tell them they put it into the wrong account?"

"Yes, Mr. John, I can try, but with cash deposits, it's difficult to know who put the money in. I will see what I can do and get back to you. But Mr. John, it will take a few hours."

"That's okay, just call me back when you find out."

"Yes, Mr. John. Is there anything else I can help you with today?"

"No, that's more than enough. Thank you."

"Thank you for calling the Oriental Banking Corporation. Have a nice day."

J ohn walked back into the office and sat down at his desk. He shivered as the chill from the air-conditioning cooled his sweat-soaked shirt.

The boss had arrived while he had been out and glared at John from inside his office, pointedly looking at his watch. John ignored him. He couldn't stand the arrogant arsehole and avoided contact with him as much as possible. John opened his email inbox and went through his emails, but he couldn't concentrate. His mind kept going back to the money in his account. Why would someone make such a big mistake? He allowed his mind to wander, to entertain thoughts of keeping the money. It wasn't a large fortune, but it would solve his current problems and allow him to make a new start. He sighed and shook his head to clear the idle thoughts. There was no point in fantasizing about what wasn't his. He focused on his email again.

It was late afternoon, just before closing when the bank called him back. John asked them to hold for a minute, muted the call, and walked out of the office, his boss' eyes drilling holes in his back. He skipped down the stairs to the toilet and locked himself in before unmuting the call.

"Hello. I'm sorry to keep you waiting."

"That's okay, Mr. John. We have checked the deposits, and there is no way of finding out who put the money into the account as they are all cash deposits. Each deposit was in a different branch, by a different person, and we don't have the means to track them down."

John frowned. "But that's crazy!" His heart raced. "Don't you require identification when someone is making a cash deposit? I thought the banks were strict now. Aren't you all worried about money laundering and terror financing?"

"Yes, Mr. John, strict regulations are in place, but the Hong Kong Monetary Authority only requires us to identify the customer if the deposit exceeds one hundred and twenty thousand dollars. All these deposits are well under the limit. I'm sorry, Mr. John, but I don't know what to suggest."

John turned, and with trembling hands, flipped the toilet seat lid down and sat on it. He couldn't believe what was happening.

"Mr. John? Are you there?"

"Yes, sorry. I was just thinking." He took a deep breath and composed himself. He spoke out loud the thought he hadn't dared to entertain earlier. "So, are you saying the money in my account now belongs to me?"

"Yes, Mr. John."

"And they can't take it back?"

"No, Mr. John. It's in your account. They can't take it back."

"Are you sure?"

"Yes." She lowered her voice, "Mr. John why worry about it? You are very lucky. Just keep the money. Whoever did it has made a mistake, but it is their problem, not yours."

"Hmmm, I suppose you are right," John nodded, forgetting she couldn't see him. He still couldn't believe it.

"Is there anything else I can do for you today?"

"No, that's all, thank you. Thank you very much."

John sat in shock. By some weird stroke of luck, he had more money in his account than he had ever had before. It wasn't a fortune, but even when he worked in the bank, he never had that much cash available. Everything he earned had gone for expenses and his lifestyle. His mind raced, filled with possibilities, but he didn't know what to do next.

The outer door handle wiggled as someone tried to enter. He ignored it. Finally, he was financially free again. He couldn't contain his excitement and jumped up off the toilet seat and punched the air with delight.

"Yes, yes, yes!"

"Hey, open the door. Let me in."

John slipped his phone into his pocket and unlocked the door. Steven from Marketing stood outside, looking annoyed.

"All yours, mate," John said with a laugh as he slapped him on the back and skipped up the stairs. He walked inside the office to his desk. He grabbed his bag, glanced around the office, then with a wave at his frowning boss, walked out the door without looking back.

7

J ohn woke late, almost ten a.m. He hadn't been able to sleep, tossing and turning until three a.m. before he finally drifted off. Thoughts on what to do with his newfound wealth, his financial freedom, had filled his mind. There was one thing that was definite—he wasn't going back to that dead-end job anymore.

Climbing out of bed, he stretched, then walked into the kitchen, opening the cupboard, removing his French Press. He took a packet of coffee powder from the fridge and measured coffee into the French Press before pouring a small amount of hot water over the ground coffee. He waited thirty seconds for the coffee to bloom, then poured in the rest of the hot water. He set his timer for four minutes and with a coffee mug, carried the French Press into the living room, placing it on the two-seater dining table. He stared out the window at the hillside that rose steeply behind his apartment building while he waited for the coffee to steep. A hiker was climbing the steep trail to the top of the hill, and John watched him, but his mind was elsewhere. He thought of the money and how Charlotte should have been there to enjoy it with him. The things they could have done together. The timer going off brought him back to the present, and he pressed the plunger on the coffee press and poured himself a mug of steaming black coffee while he thought about his next step. Should he buy something? He didn't actually need anything, and his wants weren't much. He had always wanted a nice car, perhaps a Porsche, but the traffic in Hong Kong and the cost of parking made that impractical, and it would just tie him down. More than anything, he wanted to be free. Free to make his own choices, to travel when he wanted, to do what he wanted when he wanted and not be bound to a job, chained to a desk like a modern-day slave.

He sat back in his chair and grinned. That's what this money would give him. Freedom. He drank the rest of the coffee and headed for the shower. For the first time in over a year, he was excited about the future.

8

Showered and dressed, John picked up his phone from the bedside table and powered it on, more out of habit than necessity. It wasn't like he was expecting any calls or needed to be in touch with the office anymore. He wasn't going back to work that was for sure.

The phone vibrated with message alerts, and he glanced down at the screen, scrolling through the messages and emails—a couple of spam messages selling Viagra and an email notifying him someone in Nigeria wanted to give him some money. He chuckled, amused at the irony of the situation. There was a message from his boss, asking him where he was. Just reading the message irritated him, the thought of going back to the office filling him with dread. He deleted it and moved on to the next message in the queue. It read 'number withheld,' more spam he thought as he tapped on the message window and it opened.

We've paid you. Now it's your turn to do something for us.

Strange. John sat down on the edge of his bed and looked at the screen again. Who was this, and what did they mean? Paid me? An uneasy feeling came over him. He thought for a minute, then typed:

Who is this?

He sat and waited tensely. A minute later, his phone vibrated in his hand. He opened the message.

You don't need to know who we are. Just know we have paid you, and now you must do what you have been paid for.

John frowned.

What do you mean? This is a joke, right?

The phone vibrated again almost instantly.

Do you think $1,000,000 is a joke? We are serious. You will do what you have been paid for, and if you don't, there will be serious consequences for you!

John stared at the phone. Shit. This wasn't good. All the excitement about the future disappeared, replaced with alarm. Whoever this person was, if they were prepared to pay one million to get something done, it must be more serious than running a few errands. The phone vibrated again.

We know everything about you, Mr. Hayes. Where you live, where you work, how much you earn. If you don't do what we ask, you will wish you had never been born.

A knot formed in the pit of John's stomach—a fear he hadn't felt since the incidents in Bangalore. He dropped the phone on the bed and stood. Fuck, shit, fuck! He paced around the bedroom, wishing he could rewind to the day before when he had no money in his account. What should he do? He would call the police, let them handle it. The Hong Kong Police were good—honest and efficient. They would sort it out. He paused and looked down at the phone lying on the bed. If he called the police, he would have to give up the money and go back to his shitty life. He glanced at Charlotte's photo on the bedside table.

"What should I do Charlie?" The photo remained silent.

He remembered what he had gone through to avenge Charlotte's death—the steps he had taken, the decisions he had made. Fuck it. I've been in bad situations before. It can't be any worse than that. Only one way to find out. He crossed the room and picked up the phone.

What do I have to do?

A minute later.

We knew you would come to your senses, Mr. Hayes. Wait for the next message.

The phone vibrated again. A photo.

He looked at the photo. A deeply tanned, middle-aged Westerner looked back at him, his hair expensively cut, grey at the temples. He looked familiar, full of confidence as he smiled at the camera.

It was what was written under the photo that sent a chill down John's spine.

Kill this man by Sunday.

9

The face seemed vaguely familiar. Lean and tanned, the man in the photo exuded an aura of success. He faced the camera with self-confidence and an air of satisfaction with his position in life. All of this was registering in John's subconscious, but his lizard brain, the one in charge of fight or flight, was in panic mode. He sat down again, his legs feeling weak, unable to support his weight. Was this a practical joke? It was definitely not funny. He looked at the message again. The number was withheld so he couldn't even phone them and confront them.

He typed another message.

Is this some kind of sick joke? I don't want your money. You can have it back. I will transfer it back straight away. You have the wrong person.

The phone buzzed again.

We have the right person, Mr. Hayes. You have two choices. Do what we ask and live a long life in comfort. If you don't, you too will be dead by the end of the week.

John would definitely call the police. No amount of money was worth killing anyone for. Yes, he had killed before. Those bastards deserved everything that was coming to them. They had taken the only woman he had ever loved and destroyed his life. But this was different. He had no idea who this guy was, and John had no reason to take an innocent person's life even if someone gave him a million dollars. He could never enjoy the money, knowing someone had died for it. He would call the police, tell them everything. What was the emergency number in Hong Kong? 911? 111? He had never needed it so had no idea. Before he could work it out the phone buzzed again.

Don't even think about going to the police. We will know immediately, and your life will be over.

John dropped the phone on the bed and stared at it. How did they know what he was thinking? He took a deep breath and walked out of the bedroom. In the kitchen, he grabbed a glass and filled it with cold water from the tap. His hands shook, spilling some of the water, so he put the glass down again. He took another deep breath, filling his lungs, then let the air out slowly, hoping to remove the tension. It didn't work. His heart was pounding, and despite the air conditioning, he could feel sweat forming on his forehead. Who was this and why had they chosen him? Did they know what he had done in Bangalore? Did they know he had killed before? Fuck! John banged the edge of the sink with his fist. If they did know, then he couldn't go to the police. That would be the end. Shit, shit! What should he do? His fingers tapped a nervous rhythm on the bench top as he stared out the window. He had to get a grip on himself. He could either panic and feel sorry for himself, or he could try to take control of the situation.

They said he had until Sunday to live, so that gave him some time. Not much time, but he wouldn't give up yet. No point in upsetting them now and shortening his life. He would find a way out. He walked back into the bedroom and picked up the phone. He looked at Charlotte's photo, and drawing strength from her, he typed:

Who is this person, and why do you want him killed? He hit send.

He waited, but not for long. The phone vibrated in his hand. Looking down, he read:

The why is none of your business. His name is Peter Croft. The rest is up to you. Google him. If you want to see next week, you had better start now.

10

J
ohn grabbed his laptop from beside the bed and walked into the living room where he sat again at his tiny dining table. Opening his browser, he typed in 'Peter Croft.'

Immediately, several entries came up, and John realized why he had seemed so familiar. Peter Croft was a well-known businessman in Hong Kong and a regular on the society pages. John clicked on one of the links and started reading.

Peter Croft was born in Hong Kong in 1960 to William and Susan Croft, both from England. William was working for the government in the Lands Department as a Government Surveyor. They had a comfortable life with all the perks and privileges that came with a government job in the colonies—a large apartment in Mid-Levels, a Filipina Amah, and evenings and weekends at the Jockey Club.

When he was old enough, Peter attended King George V School with all the other expatriate offspring. He was average academically, but where he excelled was on the

sports-field, representing the school in athletics and foot-
ball. He continued his activity in later life, regularly running
the trails around The Peak and playing squash once a week
at his club.

His parents had wanted him to go to a university in
England, but Peter was a young man in a hurry, not one to
waste time over a qualification when there were fortunes to
be made in the growing Colony. Fresh out of school, he
arranged an entry-level clerical position at one of the vener-
able British trading firms or "Hongs" through one of his
former classmates whose father was a director of the firm. It
wasn't long before he made his presence known through
hard work and an eagerness to learn, moving out of the clerical role into a more active position. It was real estate that
fascinated him, and he befriended the expats in the Real
Estate Division, picking their brains over beers in sleazy
Wanchai bars. After several years, he had worked his way up
to a senior position in the Real Estate Division, doing property deals on the side, leveraging his father's government
contacts and the aura surrounding his trading house's name.
He eventually decided working for someone else would
never make him truly rich and handed in his resignation,
immediately launching his own company, taking some of
his former colleagues with him. His rise since then had
been meteoric, and he was now considered one of the
largest, non-Chinese developers in the city.

John sat back and rubbed his eyes. So far, there was
nothing to suggest why someone wanted Peter killed. It all
sounded like the fairytale Hong Kong story, the sort of story
that inspired the city's population to work hard and aim for
the stars. He got up and put the kettle to boil for fresh coffee
before sitting down and reading on.

There were entries and news articles about Peter's support of the arts and various Hong Kong charities. There were photos of him and his second wife, Sylvia, a strikingly beautiful ex-Cathay Pacific air hostess, attending dinners and openings of boutiques and exhibitions. He had a house on The Peak and a luxury motor yacht moored in the Aberdeen Marina. He liked cars and had a collection the envy of many a businessman. His wife was driven around in an S Class Mercedes, from high tea to nail salon.

John heard the kettle click off and stood to prepare a fresh pot of coffee. He leaned against the kitchen counter and stared thoughtfully out the window. From everything he had read, Peter Croft was the model of a successful businessman. He had either never set a foot wrong or was brilliant at manipulating the media. There was nothing online to suggest why anyone would want him dead, and there was nothing John could find that would even justify killing him. He seemed like such a nice guy. John looked at his watch, it was after midday. He had five and a half days left. What should he do next? He wanted to see the man in the flesh; he didn't know how it would help, but he had to do something and hoped observing him would give him some ideas. Walking back to the laptop, John googled the company website and found the address and phone number. He dialed, and the phone rang twice before being answered.

"Pegasus Land, how may I direct your call?"

"May I speak to Peter Croft please?" asked John

"One moment, please."

The phone rang again before an American-accented Chinese lady answered. "Peter Croft's office."

"Hello, may I speak to Peter please?" John thought he had better sound on familiar terms.

"I'm afraid he is in a meeting at the moment. Who's calling?"

John ended the call. At least he knew Peter was in Hong Kong. He then looked up the ferry timetable. There was one leaving in twenty minutes for the Central District where Peter's office was located. John needed to get moving.

J
ohn gazed out the window as the high-speed catamaran backed away from the pier and turned, picking up speed as it passed the Disneyland Resort on the left before heading out into Victoria Harbour. He wouldn't sit around and wait to be killed. He had to figure out a way to get out of this mess but didn't have much time. Killing again was not an option. The events in Bangalore still gave him nightmares, and he didn't want to add to his tally, but he couldn't see another way out. The thirty-minute ferry journey wouldn't be long enough for him to find a solution, but he could at least observe the man, watch his movements while he worked out what to do next.

The ferry reached its cruising speed as it passed between the Tsing Ma Bridge on the left and the small uninhabited island of Kau Yi Chau on the right. Oil tankers and container ships from all over the world filled the channel, and in the distance could be seen the triple smokestacks of the Lamma Island Power Station. The view normally filled John with wonder and awe—not today. He saw nothing, his thoughts racing as the ferry veered slightly to pass an abandoned cruise liner, a former casino ship whose bankrupted owner had left it to rust away in the middle of the harbor. John had no one to confide in and no one he could trust. He certainly didn't want to end up in prison. Whatever he decided though, he would keep the money. John wouldn't experience this much stress without making it worthwhile.

John glanced around the cabin as they approached Kennedy Town on the western side of Hong Kong Island, its towering buildings emerging from the shore, the steep forest-clad hills of Pok Fu Lam and The Peak rising even higher behind them. At this time of the day, the ferry wasn't full, and most of the occupants were dozing or staring at their phones. One passenger averted his gaze as John looked in his direction, and at first, John thought nothing of it, his mind pre-occupied. But an uneasy feeling made him look back. In the same row on the other side of the ferry sat a young man in a tracksuit, reading a newspaper. He sat at an angle, facing John's direction, and each time John had looked his way, the young man's eyes had been on him and not the newspaper. John shrugged. Maybe he was paranoid, but it wouldn't hurt to keep an eye on him, just to be sure.

The boat slowed as it passed the glass and red steel twin towers of the Shun Tak Centre. Some passengers, eager to be among the first to disembark, rose and stood in the aisles. As the boat hit the chop left by the departing Hong Kong to Macau Hydrofoil, the ferry rocked and rolled, causing the standing passengers to grab the chairs and handrails for support. John sat and watched. He didn't need to be the first one off, and besides, he wanted to keep an eye on the Chinese man. In his peripheral vision, he saw he too remained seated.

The boat docked at Pier Three, and the passengers disembarked. John rose and followed them off the boat, down the ramp, through the ferry terminal, then up the steps onto the overhead walkway that led to the IFC building. Peter Croft's office was in Queens Road Central, and John knew how to get there on foot, making the maximum use of the pedestrian over-bridges and air-conditioned walkways that linked the buildings in the Central District. The less time he spent outside in the heat and humidity, the better.

He walked through the IFC Mall, past the stores selling fancy designer goods and clothing, and paused outside a menswear store, admiring the clothing in the window display. At least that's how he wanted it to look. Instead, he examined his reflection to see whether he was being followed. A few shops down stood the Chinese man, peering into the window of a store selling women's lingerie. All those hours he had spent reading spy thrillers weren't wasted. At least he had learned how to spot a tail. He didn't know what to do about it but would have to be careful in the future.

Right now, he was only visiting Peter Croft's office, something whoever was threatening him would expect him to do so there was little point in hiding. John walked on and cut through Exchange Square, then took the walkway that crossed Connaught Road before entering the air-conditioned route that led through Alexandra House and into The Landmark. He rode the escalator down to the ground floor and stepped out onto Pedder Street. He waited for the lights to change, then crossed with the crowd of office workers onto Queens Road. About a hundred meters further along, he reached the headquarters of Pegasus Land, Peter's property company. John walked inside and studied the office directory on the wall in the building's lobby. It was a thirty-story building, but

Peter's company appeared to only occupy the top three floors.

John walked back out onto the street and looked around. His Chinese follower stood across the road, staring into a jeweler's window. Based on his choice of shops, the guy was either following him or looking for a present for a girlfriend. John thought for a moment, unsure of the next step. He contemplated going up to the office but had no idea what he would do when he got there. Spotting a cafe across the road, he decided to base himself there while he thought of a plan. There was a space by the window which he reserved using a magazine from the rack by the door and ordered a coffee from the counter. He rarely drank coffee in the afternoons, it kept him hyper for too long into the night, but he figured today he might need it. Anyway, there were lots of things he was doing now he wouldn't normally do.

Sitting down by the window, he scanned the street outside, but he had lost sight of his Chinese watcher. He hoped the people he was up against were as amateurish as the guy following him. At least then, he might have a chance of outwitting them. He looked at his watch—two-thirty p.m. He settled in for a long wait.

12

Two and a half hours and three black coffees later, John watched as a black S Class Mercedes pulled up to the curb across the street. Two minutes later, he saw a man fitting Peter Croft's description exit the building and climb into the back seat.

Shit! He was going to lose him. John jumped up and left the cafe, running to the curb as the Mercedes pulled out and merged with the evening traffic. John looked around frantically and spotted a taxi pulling up on his side of the road. He ran toward it as the passenger got out. John pushed past the couple about to get in and jumped into the back seat. He pulled the door shut as they cursed him in Cantonese and told the driver to follow the Mercedes.

The driver looked at him in the mirror and raised his hands, "*Bingo ah?* What are you saying?"

John wracked his brain for the little Cantonese he could remember, conscious the Mercedes was getting away.

"*Tsek hoi, tsek hoi. Faidi la.* Go straight, go straight. Quickly"

The driver shrugged and muttered something under his breath, then pulled out into the traffic.

John peered through the windscreen, straining to see where the Mercedes had gone. He could just make out the corner of the car about six cars ahead, paused at a red light, fortunately. He was lucky it was rush hour, and the traffic was heavy. The light ahead changed, and the traffic moved again. The Mercedes indicated and turned right, headed down the hill, then turned right again onto Des Voeux Road.

"*Jun yao,* turn right," John told the taxi driver. The Mercedes made its way east along Des Voeux Road, weaving between the double-decker buses and trams. It crossed over Pedder Street and headed down Chater Road before pulling to the curb next to the back entrance of the Mandarin Hotel.

John told the taxi driver to stop, "*Lido yau lok.*" He watched as Peter climbed out of the Mercedes, straightened his jacket, and walked into the hotel.

John thrust a fifty dollar note, double the meter rate, over the front seat and climbed out, ignoring the barrage of thank yous from the previously grumpy driver.

The hotel was close to Peter's office, it would have been quicker to walk, but what was the point of being a millionaire if you can't be driven everywhere?

John crossed the footpath, pushed open the glass double doors, and entered the corridor that led from the street toward the hotel lobby. He could just see Peter turning left after the reception and entering the doorway that led to the Captain's Bar. John followed.

13

A short flight of steps led down from the lobby into the Captain's Bar. John paused at the top of the steps as his eyes adjusted to the subdued lighting and surveyed the bar. He hadn't been there in a long time and wanted to familiarize himself with the layout again before finding a spot to observe Peter Croft.

Two elderly Chinese barmen in white shirts and black ties were busy preparing drinks behind a bar running the length of the left side of the room. In front of the bar was a row of high-backed leather stools, some of them occupied, the rest of the bar filled with comfortable, red leather easy chairs and sofas arranged around tables. With its wood-paneled ceiling and framed black and white prints on the walls, the bar had the aura of a luxurious gentlemen's club.

Peter sat by himself in a booth in the far corner, staring at his phone and absentmindedly popping peanuts into his mouth from the small silver bowl in front of him. John sat on a barstool and positioned himself where he could observe Peter's reflection in the mirror behind the bar. He watched as a Filipina waitress delivered a drink to Peter's table, then realizing he needed to blend in, scanned the selection of bottles behind the bar, signaling one of the barmen.

"Yes, sir?"

"I'll have a Botanist and tonic, lots of ice, slice of orange, please."

"Excellent choice, sir."

John grinned, convinced the barman would say that to everyone. The waitress appeared at his side with two small silver bowls, one with peanuts, the other with potato chips and slid them across the bar top in front of him.

"Here you go, sir."

John turned to thank her, and she gave him a big smile. She was pretty with big eyes and caramel skin and held his gaze for a moment longer than was necessary. He looked away, feeling uncomfortable.

Since Charlotte died, he hadn't allowed himself to think about having a relationship again. The pain was still raw, keeping him awake at nights. He knew no-one could ever replace her.

His drink arrived, and he took a sip, savoring the refreshing taste of the gin, the orange slice highlighting the drink's botanicals. He nodded his approval to the barman and pulled out his phone, pretending to study it while watching Peter in the mirror.

After a couple of minutes, an overweight Chinese man in a grey suit and blue silk tie joined Peter. The suit was well cut, his shoes expensive looking and highly polished. They shook hands, and Peter beckoned to the waitress to order a drink. Once the drink arrived, they huddled together, deep in conversation. The Chinese man looked familiar to John, but he couldn't place him. He was in early middle age but balding prematurely, his hair combed over from one side in a vain attempt to hide the baldness. His short, fat fingers rapidly emptied the bowl of peanuts as his eyes darted nervously around the room.

After a while, Peter rose and walked toward the men's toilet near the back of the bar. His companion sat back in the booth and waved to the waitress, asking for more peanuts. John watched him in the mirror and couldn't shake off the feeling he had seen this man before, he just couldn't remember where or when.

The man's phone buzzed on the table, and he picked it up and answered. He frowned, and scanned the room, looking at everyone in the bar. His eyes met John's in the mirror, and he quickly looked away and ended the call. He slipped the phone back into his pocket and stood up just as Peter returned from the toilet. He whispered something to Peter before turning and hurrying to the door, leaving a puzzled-looking Peter sitting alone. Whoever it was on the call, John suspected it had something to do with him. As he sipped his drink and pondered his next move, he felt someone standing beside him. Looking up, in the mirror he saw Peter standing beside him, signaling to the barman for a drink. He caught John's eye and smiled.

"I feel I know you. Have we met?"

"I don't think so."

Peter nodded slowly, studying his face, then proffered his hand. "I'm Peter"

John hesitated, unsure about giving his real name, then rolled with it, and shook his hand.

"John."

"Hi, John. You looked familiar, and I thought our paths may have crossed. Hong Kong can be a small city," Peter grinned. "Do you mind if I join you?" He didn't wait for an answer, pulling up a bar stool and sitting down.

John eyed him warily, wondering what he should do. Here was the man someone had instructed him to kill sitting beside him. Not at all how he had expected the evening to pan out.

"Can I buy you a drink? What are you drinking?"

"Ah, thanks. Botanist and tonic."

Peter pointed at John's glass, "One of these, thanks, Alvin. In fact, make it two, it looks good."

"Certainly, Mr. Croft."

Peter turned back to John. "So, what do you do, John?"

John wasn't sure how much to tell him, so he decided on the bare minimum. "I work for a financial services company here in Central. How about you?"

"I'm in real estate," Peter replied modestly, giving no clue to his wealth and the size of the company he ran.

The drinks arrived, and Peter held his glass up. "Cheers."

John clinked his glass against his and took a sip.

"Wow, that's good," exclaimed Peter. "I've never had Botanist with an orange garnish before. It's fantastic."

John smiled. It was easy to see why Peter was a popular member of Hong Kong's social scene. He had a natural, easy-going charm, the conversation flowed, and John forgot his earlier inhibitions. Peter seemed genuinely interested in John's life, asking questions and paying attention to his answers even though John was reluctant to give too much away. It was hard for John to see why anyone would want to kill the man. The time passed quickly, John relaxing more and more as the conversation flowed, the first drink soon followed by another. Before long, Peter pulled back the cuff of his shirt and looked at the time on his gold Patek Phillipe.

"I have to go, John. I have a dinner reservation. It's been a pleasure talking to you." He stood and waved to the barman.

"Alvin, please get my friend here another drink and put it on my account."

John protested, pushing his stool back to stand up.

"No, not at all, John. It's my pleasure. I've enjoyed our chat." He reached inside his jacket and pulled out a silver card case. Opening it, he took out a business card and handed it over to John. "If you ever need anything, please feel free to give me a call. My private number is on the back."

He shook John's hand, patted him on the shoulder with his free hand, then turned and headed out of the bar.

John watched him leave and sat back down as his fresh drink arrived. He stared at the business card in his hand. He was no closer to resolving his problem, and to make matters worse, he now actually liked his target.

On the bar top, his phone buzzed. He picked it up and looked at the screen.

Enjoy your drink. You have five days left.

14

John glanced around the room, the buzz from the gin and tonics erased by the arrival of the text message. A young couple sat close together in one of the darker corners, whispering in each other's ears. Two Japanese businessmen in grey suits discussed some documents laid out on their table. To John's right, at the end of the bar, an elderly expat, his tie loosened and his sleeves rolled up, sat nodding off into his whiskey. The waitress caught his eye as he looked around and winked at him. He looked away. The two barmen busied themselves, polishing glasses and wiping down the bar top. There was no sign who had sent the text or who was watching him.

As he sat there, sipping his drink, he thought about what to do next. He was actually no further forward than yesterday, had no idea who was threatening him, and had no desire to kill Peter. He had killed before, but that was justice. Even so, it hadn't made it any easier, and the memory still kept him awake at night. There had to be another way.

John thought back over the meeting and remembered the Chinese man who had been sitting with Peter. He had definitely seemed disturbed when he took the call, and there was something familiar about the guy as if John had seen him before somewhere.

He opened the web browser on his phone and typed in 'Peter Croft.' Selecting images, he scrolled through the photos—Peter being interviewed, with his wife at a charity function, on his yacht or skiing in Europe. He had looked through about ten photos when one caught his eye—a group of businessmen in suits at a cocktail party, each of them holding a champagne glass and smiling for the camera. Peter stood on the left, his glass held high as if saying cheers. In the middle stood an elderly Chinese man in a dark suit and a white shirt, the top button undone. On the right stood the man from this evening's meeting. John looked at the caption: *Peter Croft, Ronald Yu, and David Yu at the Hong Kong Chamber of Commerce Annual General Meeting.*

John took another sip of his drink and typed *David Yu* into the search bar.

David Yu, forty-seven-year-old son of Ronald Yu, the Chairman and Founder of Golden Far East Ltd.

John clicked on another article and scanned through it. David Yu was the sole heir to the fortune his father, Ronald Yu, had built from scratch after moving to Hong Kong from Guangzhou fifty years ago with nothing but the shirt on his back. His company had investments in transportation, shipping, and real estate, and he had become one of Hong Kong's wealthiest businessmen.

David was educated at King George V School at the same time as Peter Croft and had gone on to Harvard Business School, his admission no doubt helped in no small part by a generous endowment from his father. Upon his return to Hong Kong, he had dabbled in several businesses with moderate success, some of which had to be bailed out by his father. He was a regular in the casinos in Macau, and despite his less than attractive appearance, often had a glamorous young lady on his arm. He too had a collection of exotic cars, and one of his collection of Ferraris was often spotted outside Hong Kong's restaurants and bars in the evenings.

John's gut told him there was something not right about David Yu. He must be connected, but he couldn't yet figure out how. And if he was connected, why had he chosen John? He couldn't possibly know what John had done before. There were still too many questions.

15

J ohn didn't sleep well that night, tossing and turning, his mind churning back and forth over the mess he was in. Eventually, at five a.m., he gave up the fight and got up. After a strong cup of coffee, he pulled on his running gear and went for a run, striding down the hill away from his apartment building. He took the longer route, needing the time to clear his head, to get the blood pumping through his veins. There weren't many other people awake, few lights on in the darkened buildings nearby. A couple of early morning joggers and dog walkers were out, but otherwise, the streets were quiet. The sun was yet to climb above the hills in east Kowloon, but its first rays were starting to push back the darkness. Reaching the end of Discovery Bay near the Marina Club, he doubled back and took a right turn along the beachfront. The surface of Victoria Harbour was smooth as glass, and the early morning sun's rays were turning the water shades of orange. A lone Chinese lady practiced tai chi on the beach, her movements calm and fluid. John turned back inland and headed up the hill before taking the right turn onto Seabee

Lane. He felt good—the sleepiness dispelled with the exercise-induced endorphins, his mind clear again. He had yet to come up with a solution or even an idea of what step to take next, but he felt better, ready to take on the world. He remembered when he had last been in this situation—that time back in Bangalore. Then he had four people to kill, revenge for Charlottes's murder. Even then, he had no idea how to proceed, but events had turned in his favor and opportunities had presented themselves. He was confident it would happen again—he just had to be ready. After sprinting the last five hundred meters, he walked around the garden at the foot of the building, catching his breath and trying to cool down.

Back upstairs in his apartment, after showering and changing, he thought back to the previous evening. John was convinced David Yu had been disturbed when he saw John, and that made little sense unless he was involved. A thought struck John, and he grabbed his laptop from the dining table, opening the web browser and typing in the name of Peter's company. Once the results came up, he clicked through to the website for Pegasus Land and looked at the options available on the homepage. He selected the 'About' tab and scanned the page. There was a history of the company and the usual meaningless platitudes about how Pegasus Land was striving for a better future for the citizens of Hong Kong by developing better buildings. That wasn't what John was looking for. He moved the cursor to the right and clicked on a link that read 'Leadership.' Bingo! Peter's name was at the top as Chairman and CEO, but it was the name underneath that interested John—David Yu, Managing Director. John sat back in his chair and rubbed his face. He stared blankly out the window at the hillside as his mind raced.

So, he had found the connection, but why was he nervous about seeing John at the bar? Was he the one who wanted Peter killed? If so, what did he stand to gain?

John needed to find out more. Perhaps he should follow David? He googled David and spent time scanning through the results. One headline from a few years ago caught his eye: *David Yu pays record price for a house on the Peak*

Well, if nothing else, John now knew where David lived. He looked at his watch. It was still early, so he grabbed a baseball cap and a pair of sunglasses and headed out the door. Once out on the street, he looked left and right, looking for any signs of a watcher. Two men in multi-colored lycra whizzed past on expensive road bikes. At the bus stop, a line of commuters waited, but none paid him any attention, all of them staring at their phone screens. A movement near the trees on the opposite side of the road caught his eye, and he looked closer, but it was only a dog walker cleaning up after one of the three dogs she held on a leash. Weighing his transport options, he decided on taking the bus to the railway station. He figured it would be easier to lose a tail on the train if someone was following him. Once on board, he scanned the carriage but couldn't see any sign of his watcher from the day before or anyone else taking undue interest in him. The train pulled into the inter-change at Lai King station, and John watched as a large portion of commuters disembarked to switch lines. Just as the doors started beeping, announcing their imminent closure, John leaped from the carriage onto the platform, the doors closing behind him. He looked up and down the platform as the train departed, but he was alone, no-one got off with him. He pulled on the baseball cap and donned his sunglasses before moving down the platform a little way and waited for the next train. It came just five minutes later, and he rode it all the way to Hong Kong Station, hoping his rudimentary disguise would work.

From Hong Kong Station, he took the underground passageway to Central Station and caught a train to Admiralty where he got off, crossed over to the other platform, immediately catching a train back to Central. He watched his fellow passengers in the reflection of the windows but was confident no-one was following him.

Exiting Central Station, he climbed the steps to the Landmark building, then walked outside to the taxi rank. He hailed the first taxi in the queue and gave the driver the address of a house on the same street as David Yu's.

16

D avid Yu's house was set high on the southern slope of The Peak, home to Hong Kong's super-rich. The taxi drove past the house, and John observed the property from the passenger window. High walls topped with electric wire surrounded the house, and cameras were positioned at each corner. A security guard stood outside the double height steel gate, his eyes following the taxi as it passed.

About a hundred meters farther, just after a curve in the road, John asked the taxi driver to stop and got out. He waited as the taxi drove off, then crossed the road and sat down at a bus stop where he could look back down the road and observe the house without attracting suspicion. Thick jungle lined the street on both sides, and several Banyan trees between the bus stop and David's house further shielded him from direct view. Traffic was light and pedestrians non-existent. John didn't want to stand out, so he pulled out his phone and pretended to check messages while keeping one eye on the house. It was now around nine a.m., and John hoped he wouldn't have to wait for too long, guessing David Yu would head into his office before too late in the morning. Half an hour passed before he saw activity by the gate. The security guard looked up and down the street, then pressed his earpiece and muttered something into his sleeve before pressing a button beside the gate. The gate slid open, and a silver and black Rolls Royce Phantom pulled out, checked for oncoming traffic, then slipped out onto the road. John could just make out David sitting in the back seat, looking at his phone.

John looked around for a taxi and spotted one coming down the hill toward him. He waved but saw it was already occupied. Shit, shit! John didn't want to lose the Rolls Royce. He had no other way of following the car except by taxi. He paced back and forth, then caught sight of another red taxi heading his way. He waved frantically, and as soon as it pulled over, he jumped in and instructed the driver to head downhill. The Rolls had disappeared from sight, but there was only one road down the hill, and he hoped he would pick it up before it had gone too far. Sure enough, they caught up with the car as it paused at a junction before merging onto Peak Road. John wasn't too worried about keeping a distance, Hong Kong's red taxis were everywhere, and one following behind wouldn't even be noticed. Both vehicles continued along Peak Road as it followed the contours of the slope, switching back and forth on itself as it wound its way down the hill, past huge gated villas and luxurious apartment buildings. As they neared the intersection with Guildford Road, John heard honking from behind him. He turned to look through the rear window and spotted a black Mercedes G-Wagen closing at high speed, headlights flashing. The taxi driver had seen it too and slowed, pulling to one side to let it pass. The SUV overtook them, then slammed on the brakes, swerving in front of the taxi, blocking its way as the Rolls disappeared around the next bend. The rear passenger doors opened, and two hard-faced Chinese men jumped out, dressed in black jeans and t-shirts, lurid tattoos running down their exposed forearms. One man wrenched open the driver's door and hauled the driver out, pinning him to the side of the car, gripping him by the throat. He screamed in Cantonese as the driver protested and shook his head. John sat stunned, unsure what was happening until he saw the other man move around the side of the car to his door. Shit! He didn't know what they wanted, but he wasn't about to find out. He tried locking the door on his side but couldn't find the lock. John pulled on the door handle to prevent it being opened, but the man outside was strong and had the benefit of leverage. John gave up, let go of the door handle and slid across the seat to the other side. The Chinese man grabbed him by the ankle and pulled. John kicked out with his free leg, catching him hard on the wrist. He grunted, and his grip loosened. Cursing, he reached in again with both hands but couldn't get a grip as John kicked out. John fell backward as the door behind him opened, and the other man, having released the driver, grabbed him by the hair and hauled him out of the car, throwing him onto the road. He kicked John in the stomach, and John gasped in pain, curling into a fetal position to protect himself. Both men kicked him, shouting something in Cantonese. John couldn't understand and tried to make himself as small as possible, curling tight to protect his midsection and his head.

"Stop, stop," he cried out, but the blows continued. He felt a pair of hands grab the back of his shirt, dragging him to his feet, throwing him against the side of the taxi.

Thug Number 1 held him by the throat and glared at John, his face just inches away. "Why you follow?"

"I'm not following anyone," John protested.

"You follow. We see you outside the house! You stop now! We see you again, we kill you."

He released John's throat, and before John could react, punched him hard in the stomach. John doubled over and dropped to his knees, retching onto the tarmac. Thug Number 2 put his foot against John's back and pushed him over, onto the ground. John felt hands pulling his wallet out from his back pocket. He turned to protest and watched as Thug 2 rifled through it and removed his Hong Kong Identity Card. He passed it to Thug 1 who removed his phone from his pocket and took a photo of the ID card, then threw it down beside John's head.

"*Tee seen gweilo*," he cleared his throat and spat on the ground in front of John. "Crazy white guy." Both men turned and walked toward the SUV. As they passed the taxi driver, Thug 2 feinted a punch and laughed as the driver ducked. Without looking back, they climbed into the SUV and sped away with a screech of tires.

The taxi driver rushed to John's side and helped him to his feet.

"Very bad men," he said. "*Sun Yee On*."

John winced as he stood up, pain radiating through his body. "What does that mean?"

The driver shook his head as he dusted off John's shirt. "Triad. Be careful."

17

John needed to think and clean himself up. He didn't know where else to go, so he asked the taxi driver to drop him off outside Thapa's coffee shop. The taxi driver refused to take any money from him, once again exhorting him to be careful.

John looked up and down the street to see if anyone was watching him, then climbed the steps that led to Thapa's cafe and pushed the door open.

"Good morning, John," Thapa called out, a welcoming smile on his face which disappeared as soon as he took a good look at John.

"What happened to you?"

"I got out of the wrong side of the bed. Can I use your bathroom?"

"Sure, my friend, the door at the back there."

John walked to the back, down a small corridor stacked with boxes of coffee supplies, and pushed open the door at the rear. Latching the door behind him, he turned on the tap and looked in the mirror. His face didn't look too bad—his lower lip was cut, the blood drying into a scab, traces of dirt smudged his cheeks and forehead, and his hair needed tidying. But when he lifted his shirt, he winced. Bruises covered his body, the skin turning shades of green and purple. These guys had been clever. They had wanted to send a message but not have the effects on display for all to see. John splashed water on his face and tamed his hair before gingerly tucking his shirt back in. It wasn't the first time someone had beaten him up, and he knew from experience, the bruises would fade with time. But it was about time he learned how to defend himself. He checked his appearance once more in the mirror, then unlatching the door, walked back out into the cafe.

"Here you go, John, on the house." Thapa handed him a mug of black coffee and turned to the girl working beside him.

"Celia, look after the counter for me." Celia smiled and nodded.

Thapa wiped his hands on a cloth and walked around the counter to join John at the table he had found in the corner.

"Now, do you want to tell me what happened?"

John looked around the small cafe. Apart from Celia and a customer paying for their coffee, the cafe was empty. John waited until the customer left, and Celia busied herself cleaning the coffee machine. He took a deep breath and turned to Thapa who was sitting patiently, watching his face.

"A couple of guys decided they didn't like the look of me."

"Where did it happen? Did you call the police?"

"No, I didn't, but it doesn't matter. I can look after myself. It's not the first time."

"Okay. If you say so." Thapa regarded him doubtfully. "But let me know if I can help with anything."

Despite striking up a friendship with Thapa over the past year, John still didn't know how much he could trust him. He seemed like a decent guy, but John wasn't sure how much he should share. He took a sip on his coffee, wrestling with the decision. Thapa looked back calmly, giving him time. John put the coffee mug down on the table and looked directly at Thapa.

"Have you heard of *Sun Yee On*?"

Thapa raised an eyebrow. "What have you got yourself into?"

"Oh, nothing, just something someone said."

Thapa nodded, not convinced. "*Sun Yee On* is a Triad. Do you know what Triads are, John?" He didn't wait for an answer. "Very bad people. They run all sorts of illegal activities here on the Island and in Kowloon. They don't mess around." Thapa paused, studying John's face. "I think there is something you're not telling me, John." It was a statement, not a question. John looked down at his coffee, not answering.

"John, if you are involved in any way with these people, you have to be very careful because they will think nothing of killing you if you get on their wrong side. I know, I grew up with these guys in Kowloon. They don't mess around. They rule by fear and can never show the slightest sign of weakness."

John looked up and regarded Thapa for a moment, thinking over what he had just said.

"Are you still in touch with any of them?"

Thapa looked back, the cogs and wheels in his mind visibly turning. He looked over at Celia, busy washing the coffee cups. He leaned forward and lowered his voice.

"I know some people, John, in a rival Triad, but you really shouldn't get involved with any of them. Stay away from these people."

John nodded and looked over Thapa's shoulder, toward the street. People walked past the window, caught up in their mundane lives of emails, meetings, and office politics. John took a deep breath and looked back at Thapa.

"I need your help, Thapa. I am in big trouble."

18

In a low voice, John explained what had happened in the last two days. Thapa listened without saying a word, and when John finished, he sat back in his chair and studied the wall behind John's head. After a few minutes, he leaned forward.

"I think you need to be careful about David Yu. Something doesn't sound right. I'll ask around and see if anyone knows more about him." He turned to the counter. "Celia, you can take a break now. I'll look after everything. Come back in an hour."

"*M goi sai*, Thapa, thank you." She smiled, removed the apron from her waist, and grabbed her purse and phone from beneath the counter before walking out the door.

Thapa walked to the door and locked it, smiling apologetically at a customer about to enter, then flipped the open sign to closed. He fixed a fresh coffee for John, then removed his phone from the back pocket of his jeans and dialed.

For the next thirty minutes, Thapa worked the phone, asking question after question, switching effortlessly from Cantonese to Nepalese to Hindi and back again while John drank his coffee. John couldn't follow the conversation, his knowledge of Cantonese limited to giving directions to a taxi driver, and he didn't remember much Hindi from his time in India. Instead, he used the time to clear his head. He realized there wasn't much he could do until he had gathered more information. He had to trust his subconscious to come up with a solution, and it couldn't do that unless he gave it time. He sat back in his chair, closed his eyes, and let the sound of Thapa's conversation wash over him. After thirty minutes, Thapa ended the call he was on and moved back to the table, sitting down again in front of John. John opened his eyes and looked at Thapa's face. He had a thoughtful expression on his face and a glint in his eye.

"Well?"

"The rumor is your friend David is having some money problems."

"Really, I thought he was supposed to be super rich?"

"Well, yes, but he has some naughty habits. Apparently, he has a taste for baccarat and expensive ladies from Central Europe. According to my sources, he has dropped large sums at the tables in Macau and has borrowed money from some nasty people."

"What kind of sums are we talking about?"

"Apparently millions."

"Hmmm, okay." John leaned back and gazed out the window. "But why would a successful businessman do something so stupid? He has all the money he needs, a beautiful house on the Peak, a stable of expensive cars. Why blow it all gambling?"

Thapa nodded. "It makes little sense to you or me, John, but gambling is a disease. Hong Kong people are always gambling. Look how the stock market goes up and down. Half the people have no idea what they are buying. They see the shares go up, and they jump in. David Yu is no different." Thapa gave a wry smile. "But perhaps if he stuck to shares, he wouldn't be in such a mess."

"His father has more than enough money to bail him out, surely?"

"John, David Yu's father is old school. He is a self-made man who built himself up from nothing. The story goes that at the age of fifteen he swam for two days across the water from China to Hong Kong in search of a better life. He is a tough, hard man who has been very successful and rules his company with an iron fist. David, on the other hand, has never known hardship, was born into luxury, and hasn't proven himself in business. Most of the businesses he has started have failed, or his father has bailed him out. Compared to his father, he is a failure. Do you think he would run to him to tell him he has lost millions in Macau?"

"No, I suppose you're right," John pursed his lips and nodded. "But if it is him behind the murder threat, why does he want to have Peter killed?"

"I have no idea, John. Absolutely no idea. But you need to find a way to get out of it."

19

A fter sitting with Thapa, John went for a walk to clear his head. Movement always helped him think more clearly, especially running, but he was in the middle of the city so a walk would have to suffice. He headed downhill toward Queen's Road, then turned and climbed the steep hill toward the Foreign Correspondents Club before turning right along Wyndham Street. The lunch rush was starting, and the bars and restaurants along Wyndham Street were filling up. But John wasn't hungry, his mind on more important things than food. He couldn't fit the pieces of the puzzle together. Nothing made any sense.

If David Yu was the man behind the messages, why would he want Peter Croft killed? What did he stand to gain? John remembered reading in some mystery novel or other you should "follow the money." If what Thapa's contacts said were true, David had a gambling problem and was heavily in debt. Therefore, would he gain financially by Peter's death? Would his death give him control of the company? There had to be some major benefit, otherwise he wouldn't waste a million dollars on it, especially if he was already in debt. John shook his head in frustration. He didn't know enough about company law to understand the implications, and even if he figured that out, why had David Yu chosen him? He paused at the Mid-Levels escalator, unsure which way to go. The streets were becoming increasingly crowded as workers poured out of their offices in search of a bite to eat, so he headed against the pedestrian flow and went downhill, taking the path through the lanes that ran under the overhead walkway and escalator. John reached Queen's Road again and turned right, heading back toward Pedder Street. He had no idea where he was going, just wandered aimlessly, filling in time while his subconscious did the work. His progress was much slower now, the footpaths packed with people. Spotting a gap in the traffic, he jogged across the road to the marginally less crowded northern side, grimacing as the movement reminded him of his beating. As he weaved his way through the oncoming pedestrians, he thought he heard his name being called. He looked around but couldn't see who was calling him and assumed he had misheard.

"John."

A waving hand caught his eye, and he spotted Peter climbing out of his Mercedes parked at the curb.

John pushed his way through the crowds toward Peter and held out his hand. With both hands, Peter grasped his and greeted him warmly.

"We meet again. How are you?"

"Good thanks, Peter, and yourself?"

"Excellent. I didn't expect to see you again so soon." Peter looked him up and down, noticing his casual dress. "Day off today?"

"Yes, it's a quiet week, and I had a few errands to run."

"What happened to your face?"

John's hand went to his cut lip. "Oh, I ah... walked into a door at home."

"Ouch. Sounds painful. Hey, do you have any plans this evening? My wife is out of town, we can meet up for a drink and a bite to eat."

John couldn't think of an excuse fast enough, and besides, the more he got to know Peter, the easier he might get himself out of this mess.

"Yeah, sure, I'm free. What time?"

"I've got a couple of late meetings, but why don't you pop by my office at seven, and we can leave from here." He pointed at the building behind John. John turned and realized he was outside Peter's office.

He turned back and smiled, "Sure, see you at seven."

Peter patted him on the shoulder and headed through the crowds toward his office while John looked at his watch. Plenty of time for him to go home, freshen up, and change.

20

A t seven o'clock on the dot, John walked into the building that housed the offices of Pegasus Land.

He waited for the lift, and when it arrived, stepped aside as it disgorged its load of office workers heading home after a hard day's work.

Once empty, he stepped inside, pressed the button for the thirtieth floor, and stood back, watching the numbers on the screen above the keypad as the lift ascended. He felt nervous and checked his reflection in the lift's shiny steel doors. He had put on his best casual shirt and pants in a vain attempt to match Peter's sartorial style. He didn't have the same budget as Peter, but it would have to do.

The lift doors opened on the thirtieth floor, and John walked out into a spacious, wood-paneled lobby. Directly in front of him, a Nepalese security guard sat behind a polished wooden counter. Behind him on the wall hung a large abstract canvas. John didn't recognize the work or the artist, but he was sure it was expensive. He walked toward the counter, and the guard looked up and got to his feet.

He smiled, "Can I help you, sir?"

"Ah yes, I'm here to see Peter Croft. My name is John."

"Certainly, sir, just one moment."

John looked him over as he picked up the phone and dialed an internal number. He was a smart man maybe in his early fifties and looked like he was an ex-Gurkha, still fit with a military-style haircut.

Replacing the phone, he looked up at John. "Please follow me, sir."

He led John to a door to the right of the counter and punched in a code on a keypad. The keypad beeped, and the ex-Gurkha pushed open the door and stepped inside, waiting for John to follow him. He pointed down the corridor.

"The office at the end there, sir."

John smiled his thanks and walked along the corridor. Modern art, similar to the one hanging in the reception area, lined the wall to his left, and to his right, glass partitions gave a view of rows of cubicles, most of the desks empty, the computers shut down. A window on the far side looked out across the skyline of the Central District, the towering buildings lit up like fairy lights.

As John reached the full-height glass wall at the end of the corridor, he could see Peter sitting inside, on the phone, deep in conversation. He noticed John approaching and waved him inside. John walked in, closing the door behind him. Peter smiled and pointed toward the leather couch near the window. He mouthed "Sorry" and continued with his conversation. John looked around. The view through the floor to ceiling windows was sensational, the office having clear lines of sight across Victoria Harbour toward Kowloon. The highest building, the ICC on the Kowloon side, took center stage, its top shrouded in clouds while the light show on its facade portrayed eagles and rabbits, clouds and thunderstorms. John could watch it for hours and marveled at the technology that created such an effect. He doubted he would get any work done if the office had been his, preferring to gaze out the window all day at the ever-changing view. He switched his attention down toward the harbor where sampans jostled for space with inter-island ferries and fishing boats, the harbor full of activity whatever the time of day.

"Amazing, isn't it?"

John turned toward Peter, a big grin on his face. "Yeah, I never tire of the Hong Kong skyline. It's like Bladerunner meets Gotham City."

"Ha, you're right," Peter grinned. "Sometimes, it's a little too distracting." He picked up the phone again, "I've just got to make one more call, I'm sorry."

"That's okay."

Peter wedged the phone between his shoulder and his chin as he shuffled through a pile of files on his desk. He spoke into the phone, "One moment please," then covered the mouthpiece with his spare hand and looked up at John.

"Could you do me a favor? I need a file, and I think it's in the next office." Peter gestured to the wall behind John. "Can you please grab it for me? It should be on the desk and will be labeled 'Central Reclamation.' I would have asked my assistant, but she already left for the day."

"Sure." John got to his feet and opened the door, turned right and walked to the other office. It was a similar size and layout to Peter's. A full-height glass wall separated it from the corridor, and expansive windows looked west toward the skyline of Sheung Wan and Kennedy Town. Apart from the view, it was almost a carbon copy of Peter's office with the same padded leather sofa, coffee table, and large abstract canvas on the rear wall. John opened the door and walked over to the desk. On the top was a phone and a pile of files, but it was a photo in a silver frame that caught his eye. Two Chinese men in suits smiled back at the camera. One he recognized from the photo he had seen online as Ronald Yu. The other was his son David.

He put the frame down and took another look at the room. Behind the desk was a cabinet with a large-scale model of a Ferrari FXX in a glass case. Beside it were more photos of David Yu, shaking hands with Hong Kong politicians, and a couple with him and Peter together, cutting ribbons or looking at plans. He looked back at the files on the desk. A large manila folder sat on top, and he looked at the tab to check it was the one Peter wanted. As he picked it up, loose papers fell to the floor.

John bent down and gathered them up and was about to place them back on the desk when he realized what they were—deposit slips. He looked closer—deposit slips for Oriental Banking Corporation. He started to get a bad feeling. He checked the amount—fifty thousand dollars. He checked the one underneath—fifty thousand dollars. The next one was the same. He checked the dates. All of them had the same date—Saturday's date. He looked at the account number. It looked like his, but he wasn't sure. It couldn't be a coincidence but he had to check. Placing the file back on the desk, he pulled out his phone. He scrolled across the screen until he found his banking app and logged in. He crosschecked his bank account number with the account number on the deposit slips... It was the same.

"Found it?" he heard Peter call from the neighboring office.

"Got it," he replied and put his phone back in his pocket, replaced the deposit slips, and picked up the file. He looked around the room once more, then walked out the door and back to Peter's office. Peter was still on the phone and smiled as John handed over the file. He held up two fingers and leafed through the file before continuing his conversation, something about plot ratios.

John sat back down and zoned out, his mind working overtime, thinking over what he had just seen. David Yu was definitely the man behind it all. But why would he want Peter killed?

21

Peter ended his call and looked over at John. "Thank you, John. My partner and I are working on a proposal for the Central Reclamation at the moment, and it's keeping us very busy. A lot of regulations to satisfy."

"Who's your partner?" He knew the answer, just wanted to hear it from Peter.

"David Yu. Do you know him?"

John shook his head.

"His photo is always in the magazines. He likes his Ferraris," Peter grinned. "Let's get out of here. Come back to my place, Sylvia is out of town. I'll get my staff to prepare dinner for us, and we'll have a couple of drinks."

"Sounds good."

They walked out the door, John following Peter down the corridor to the reception. He opened the door, waited until John walked through, then followed him out.

He spoke to the guard, "Rai, have Samuel bring the car around."

"Yes, sir. Good night, sir."

They rode the lift down in silence while Peter scrolled through his phone, then walked out onto the street. The S Class Mercedes was waiting at the curb, a stocky Chinese man standing beside it. He opened the door, and John climbed in while Peter walked around to the other side. John stretched out his legs and settled back in the soft leather seat. In front of him was a touch screen, and to his left, a wide armrest separated his seat from Peter's. He could get used to this, it was like sitting in a business class seat on a plane. The driver climbed in and started the engine.

"Home please, Samuel."

"Yes, sir."

Peter and John busied themselves with small talk as the car left the Central District, turned right past the Lippo Centre, and headed uphill along Cotton Tree Drive before turning onto Magazine Gap Road and climbing higher. The traffic thinned out as they climbed, and the cars became more expensive—Bentleys, Mercedes and BMWs, and John spotted a Ferrari and a McLaren racing into town for a night out.

The Mercedes pulled up outside a large gate and waited as it rolled open before driving inside. The car pulled up in front of the entrance door, and Peter got out. John opened his door, climbed out, and looked around as the gate rolled silently to a close behind them. The driveway was small, just enough for a couple of cars and led off to a triple garage on the right. The garage doors opened as the Mercedes moved toward it, and John's jaw dropped as he saw the cars parked inside. On the right was a bright yellow Porsche 964 RSR, one John had lusted after since he was a teenager. In the center garage was a forest green Porsche 959. Both were rare cars and worth millions of dollars. Peter saw John staring and smiled.

"My babies. Do you want to take a look?"

John didn't wait, he was already walking toward them.

"My partner likes his Ferraris, but I'm a Porsche man myself. You can't beat German engineering."

John walked around the RSR, his eyes running admiringly over the curved wheel arches and the large rear wing.

"1993 964 RSR, 350 horsepower. Only 51 ever built."

John couldn't believe it. He looked up at Peter. "She's beautiful." He walked over to the 959. "I saw one of these years ago in England. A silver one. I never thought I would see one in Hong Kong. The color is beautiful."

"This one has had a bit done to it. There's a company in the U.S. that updates them. I had it stripped down to bare metal and restored. It now puts out over 760 horsepower."

"You're kidding! What did it have when it was new? 400?"

"450. You know your Porsches, John."

"I've been a fan since I was a kid."

"We'll go for a drive one weekend, but now I'm parched." Peter patted him on the shoulder. "Let's go inside."

John dragged himself away from the cars and followed Peter to the front door.

Peter pushed open the oversized, wooden entrance door and walked inside. John followed him and stopped, the view in front of him taking his breath away. The view from Peter's office had been impressive, but the view from his home was something else. The full-height picture windows opened out onto the full expanse of the Hong Kong skyline and Victoria Harbour. Spread out below were the skyscrapers of Central and Wanchai, glistening and twinkling. Beyond them, Victoria Harbour curved away in a semi-circle, and across the harbor lay the expanse of Tsim Sha Tsui and

Kowloon with the darkened peaks of Lion Rock and the New Territories beyond.

"Wow," was all John could think of to say.

Peter laughed. "Come on in." He led John to the left where the entrance opened onto a wide living room furnished tastefully in cream and black. It shared the entrance lobby's view, and sliding doors opened out onto a pool deck with a four-lane wide swimming pool, cantilevered over the side of the cliff.

"Take a seat, John," Peter waved to a cluster of sofas in the middle of the room. "Imelda," he called out.

A middle-aged Filipina emerged from a side door. "Good evening, sir."

"Imelda, can you fix us some drinks, please?" He turned to John, "Botanist, tonic, and a slice of orange?"

Yes, please," John grinned. This guy was good. "You have a good memory."

"Make that two, Imelda."

"Yes, sir."

"John, come out and look at the view." Peter walked over and opened the sliding doors, stepping out onto the pool deck. John followed him outside and peered over the edge at the jungle-clad slope forty feet below. Peter watched him, a smile on his face. "It took some major engineering to do this, but it's pretty amazing, isn't it?"

John swallowed, hoping the engineer's calculations had been correct and forced a smile.

"Come over here." Peter was like a kid showing off his toys. He beckoned John over to join him at the extreme end of the deck. John walked over and tried not to think about what wasn't below him.

"Don't you love this city?" Peter waved at the view. "There isn't a better view in the world."

John had to agree. It would have been spectacular during the day, but at night, it was a multicolored fairytale of lights spread out before them. The temperature was much cooler than on the city streets below, and a gentle breeze rippled through the stand of potted heliconias lining the sides of the pool deck.

"It's incredible."

Peter turned and leaned against the handrail, looking back toward the house.

"When I was growing up, John, I promised myself one day I would have a house up on The Peak, and... Lady Luck has been kind."

Imelda arrived with the drinks, and Peter waited until John had his before raising his glass. "Cheers, John."

"Cheers," John replied and took a sip. He licked his lips, "Delicious. I'm sure it was more than just luck, Peter. I think you are being modest. Skill and hard work must have had something to do with it."

"You are too kind, John," Peter laughed. "Yes, it was a lot of hard work but worth it. You get nothing without hard work." He took a large swig of his drink. "This is delicious. Thanks for introducing me to it."

John smiled and took another sip himself. He couldn't help but like the guy. He was easy to talk to, and despite the trappings of wealth, not at all arrogant.

"Come, I'll show you around." Peter led him inside and gave him a guided tour around the house. The living room led to a separate dining room filled with an eight-seater table and chairs. At one end of the room was a well-stocked bar, and behind the bar, a door opened into a temperature-controlled wine cellar, the walls lined floor to ceiling with racks of wine bottles.

Another door led into the large, fully equipped kitchen

where Imelda and another Filipina were preparing dinner. Stairs from the living room led down to the accommodation floor which held three expansive bedrooms with ensuite bathrooms, then the floor below that contained the master suite which took up the whole bottom floor of the house. The furnishings were expensive but tasteful, nothing garish or over the top. John could imagine himself living the same way if he ever came into money. Seeing the luxurious furnishings reminded him of why he was there.

He had come into some money, but it came with strings attached, and it was those strings he needed to deal with. The thought sobered him, and he followed Peter back upstairs to the living room where a second drink was waiting. He didn't want to kill Peter. He was too nice, and he couldn't think of any justification for taking his life. Peter had done nothing but show him generosity and kindness. John didn't know what to do. He sat down, drained his drink, and picked up the fresh glass, tuning back into Peter's conversation.

After some time, they moved to the dining room for a beautifully prepared, three-course meal, Peter switching to a bottle of Penfolds Bin 95 Grange with his food, John sticking to gin. Red wine gave him a headache.

Peter's tongue loosened as he relaxed with the drinks, and over dinner, he described how he had built his company and the pressures of doing business in Hong Kong. He let it slip things weren't going so well with Sylvia, his second wife, one of the reasons she was away in Singapore. He fell silent for a while, staring at his plate. John didn't know what to say or how to comfort him. John knew what it was like to lose someone and felt sorry for him.

Peter was a nice guy, but despite all his success, perhaps

a little lonely. All most people wanted was companionship and someone to love.

John changed the subject to lighten the mood, and the conversation moved on to travel and cars, discovering they had many similar interests. John was enjoying himself and had to keep reminding himself why he was there. After dinner, they returned to the living room. The conversation paused while Imelda served them both a glass of Port, John reluctant to mix his drinks, but at the same time, not wishing to turn down Peter's hospitality. In that time, John made a decision. He waited until Imelda left the room, then put his glass down on the coffee table and leaned forward.

"Peter, I have something I must tell you."

"What, are you gay?" he laughed.

"Ha, no," he paused. "But it's serious."

Peter stopped laughing and put his glass down. "Okay."

"Last night when we met in The Captain's Bar..."

"Yes?"

John took a deep breath.

"I was following you."

22

J ohn told Peter the whole story, from the discovery of the money in his account, right up to the deposit slips found in David's office. He left nothing out, and Peter just listened, his eyes not leaving John's. When John finished, Peter sat back in his chair and let out a long exhalation of air, shaking his head in disbelief.

"Wow."

John sat back too, a huge weight off his chest.

They sat in silence for a while, Peter thinking, his eyes flicking back and forth around the room. When he spoke, it was almost as if he was speaking to himself, and John had to strain to hear him.

"If I die, David gains control of the company. He gets everything... the greedy son of a bitch. I always had my doubts about him and some of his connections, but sometimes, you can't be choosy about your bed partners."

John cleared his throat. "I've heard he has heavy gambling debts."

Peter nodded, still deep in thought. John sipped on his port, not wishing to disturb the thought process.

Suddenly, he turned to John. "I think you should do it."

"What?"

"I think you should kill me."

23

J ohn spent the night at Peter's. Peter had Imelda prepare the guest room and gave him a change of clothes for the next day.

John woke around seven, his head heavy from the gin he had consumed. He felt tired, but he couldn't sleep anymore. He thought back over the previous night's discussion and Peter's suggestion to go ahead with it. At first, he thought he was crazy, but Peter had explained they would arrange it so David was implicated in the attempted murder. Peter had a plan.

John climbed out of bed and opened the blinds. He stretched and rubbed his eyes as he looked out across Victoria Harbour toward the blue hills of the New Territories. He could get used to this lifestyle... as long as he didn't have to keep going around killing people.

He stripped off in the bathroom and examined his bruises in the mirror. His torso looked like it had been hit by a truck. He probed his abdomen with his fingertips. It was sore, very sore, but it would heal. After a long hot shower in the capacious bathroom, he felt much better, more mobile.

He splashed himself liberally with the expensive cologne left on the counter before dressing in the clothes Peter had lent him. They fit him well, both keeping themselves in shape and being of similar builds. He walked out into the bedroom and picked up his phone from the bedside table— a message had come in while he was in the shower. He tapped on the screen and opened the message app.

Don't get too comfortable. You only have four days left.

Shit. John's heart pounded, and he looked around the room before realizing how stupid that was. He wouldn't find the sender in the bedroom. He took a couple of deep breaths and calmed himself. Hopefully, this would end soon.

Not sure what to do next, he climbed the stairs to the top floor and looked around. The smell of fresh coffee and bacon came from the kitchen, so he followed his nose. Peter was already there, sitting at the breakfast bar, reading the South China Morning Post while Imelda busied herself at the stove. A small television played in the corner, the screen filled with a talking head discussing the financial markets while a ticker tape ran across the bottom of the screen.

"Good morning."

Both Imelda and Peter turned and smiled.

"Good morning, sir."

"Morning, John. Sleep well?"

John pulled out a bar stool and joined Peter at the breakfast bar. "Like a log. Been up long?"

"An hour or so. I like to exercise before starting the day. Coffee?"

"That will be great. Thanks."

Imelda prepared a coffee at the fancy stainless-steel coffee machine on the counter and brought it over.

"What would you like to eat, sir?"

John looked around the kitchen. "That bacon smells good. Bacon and eggs?"

"Sure, sir," she smiled and went back to the stove.

John pushed his phone across the bench-top toward Peter, the message open on the screen.

Peter glanced down at the screen and raised his eyebrows. He folded the newspaper and pushed it to one side. He looked at John, then flicked his eyes toward Imelda before looking back.

"Let's continue last night's conversation after breakfast. I have some ideas."

John nodded as Imelda placed a plate of fried eggs and bacon in front of him. He looked questioningly at Peter.

"I don't eat breakfast. Only coffee for me. But please tuck in."

John didn't wait any longer. He was starving.

L ater, Peter led him out onto the pool deck and closed the French doors from the house behind him.

"It's best we're not overheard," he explained. "Grab a seat." He pulled up a cane chair and gestured for John to do the same. Sitting down, they both gazed at the view in silence. The air was cool, the sun beginning its climb above the hills in East Kowloon, a gentle breeze blowing across the pool deck. The peaks of the New Territories were just hidden behind tendrils of soft clouds.

Peter broke the silence. "I've made some calls, John. I have some contacts in the police."

John stiffened. "They told me not to involve the Police."

"It's okay, I trust my guy. You have nothing to worry about."

John pursed his lips, not convinced.

"He's on his way here. I have an idea John, and with his help, we can make it work."

John looked out across the harbor. He didn't like getting too many people involved, it opened up too many possibilities for things to go wrong. He preferred to trust his own abilities and street smarts. That's how he had got away with his revenge killings in India. The difference was, this time, he didn't want to kill anyone. He liked Peter, he was a good man and didn't deserve to die.

In India, he was successful because he was the only person in the world who knew for sure what he had done there. But now, Peter knew about the messages and the money and who knows how many police would find out now. The other danger was if David Yu knew about Bangalore. The Hong Kong Police could find out and inform their counterparts in India. John would have solved one problem only to be thrown into a deeper one. He thought fast. He was screwed either way.

Peter was looking at him waiting for a response. He had to make a decision and didn't have the luxury of time to consider all the options. John bit his lip. One step at a time. He would go with the flow and see how things panned out. If the Bangalore issue came up, he would deal with it then. Hopefully, it could all be turned around, they would apprehend the man behind all this, and John could live the rest of his life in peace, a million dollars richer.

"Okay," he shrugged, "what's the plan?"

"Let's wait until Joseph gets here." He turned as they heard the French doors opening. "Ah, speak of the devil."

John turned to look at the man who had just walked onto the pool deck. A medium height Chinese in tan cargo pants and a black cotton shirt walked toward Peter, holding out his hand, his mouth smiling, but his eyes darted nervously back and forth from John to Peter.

Peter shook his hand like a politician, clasping Joseph's hand with both of his, then turned to John.

"John, this is Inspector Joseph Wong from the Organized Crime and Triad Bureau, Wanchai."

Joseph held out his hand, his eyes glancing at John's cut lip. "What happened to your face?"

John's hand moved to his lip, but before he could reply, Peter interjected, "He walked into a door. Please, take a seat."

John shook his hand as Joseph frowned at him, apparently not convinced by Peter's explanation. John studied him as he sat down, and Peter explained what had happened to John over the past few days. Joseph looked fit, no trace of a belly, his close-cropped hair greying at the temples. He listened closely to Peter, interjecting once or twice to check a fact, the fingers on his right hand tapping rhythmically on his thigh. He didn't look like a policeman— at least John's idea of how a policeman should look—and although he couldn't put his finger on it, for some reason, he didn't like him. Something about him made him uneasy. There was no warmth like he had felt when he met Peter.

Peter turned to John, including him in the conversation. "John found the deposit slips in David's office. We're sure it's him. My plan is for John to proceed as if he is going along with David's plan, and we get David involved and catch him red-handed."

John looked away from Peter and at Joseph, catching him staring at him. Joseph flicked his eyes away and sat forward.

"Let's do it on the boat."

Peter nodded slowly, frowning as he thought it over.

"Not a bad idea."

"Boat?" John questioned.

"Peter has a boat at the Aberdeen Marina. We can wire it up for sound and hidden cameras. It's an environment we can control. We'll arrange for you to be on the boat, and I'll hide on the boat with my colleagues, ready to arrest David once we have his confession. He won't be able to get away."

"But how will you get him and me on the boat at the same time?"

"That's easy," Peter replied. "I invite him on the boat all the time. I'll call him for a meeting about the Central Reclamation development. He won't know you're there. Once we are settled in, you can appear, and we'll confront him."

John nodded, playing the scenario out in his mind. He didn't like it, but he couldn't see any other way out—he had no other options.

"Let's plan it for Saturday afternoon. That will give Joseph time to wire up the stateroom on the boat and get his men ready. I often take the boat out on the weekend, anyway so it won't look suspicious."

"We'll aim for one p.m. I'll have the boat ready by then," replied Joseph. He turned to John. "Peter will give you the details, but I want you on the boat by eleven thirty to reduce the chance of anyone seeing you. You never know where his spies are."

Peter stood. "Great, it's done." He turned to John. "John, go home and get some rest. We'll need you in top form on Saturday. I'll sort out the finer details with Joseph. Why don't we all meet tomorrow morning to go through the plan once more? I'll send my driver to pick you up from the ferry."

"That sounds good." John stood and shook Peter's hand.

Joseph remained seated, watching him closely. "Thank you, Peter."

"Not at all, John." Peter clapped him on the shoulder. "Thank you for confiding in me. You are saving my life. My driver will drop you at the ferry. Rest up, and we'll speak soon."

"Thank you. That's kind of you."

"It's the least I can do. I owe you my life."

John smiled and frowned at the same time, then nodded at Joseph before walking toward the house. He slid open the door and stepped inside, sliding it closed behind him. He looked back at the pool deck. Both Peter and Joseph stared back at him, neither of them saying a word.

24

J ohn sat back, leaned his head against the headrest, and closed his eyes as the S Class Mercedes wound its way down Magazine Gap Road toward Central and the ferry piers. John had decided to go home. It was out of his hands now, nothing more he could do. He was set on a path—there was no turning back. All would come to an end on Saturday. Hopefully, it would end well.

He must have drifted off because it seemed like only seconds later the Mercedes pulled up alongside Ferry Pier Three, and the driver turned in his seat.

"Here okay, sir?"

John opened his eyes and looked around. "Ah yes, thank you."

He opened the door, climbed out, and looked at his watch as the Mercedes glided silently away. There was still another twenty minutes before the next ferry, so he walked along the footpath to a street vendor and bought a bottle of water. He twisted off the cap and took a long pull on the bottle. He felt uneasy, a prickling at the base of his neck as if he was being watched. He looked around at the passersby, but no-one seemed to pay him any attention. He glanced back at the street vendor, an elderly man, but he was busy fiddling with the knob on his transistor radio, trying to find a station. John took another sip from his bottle, but the feeling remained. He raised his vision, scanning further afield. Everyone looked normal as if they belonged, all busy going about their daily routines. A taxi pulled up in front of the taxi rank, and John watched as a young mother struggled to get out with her two young children and remove a push-chair from the trunk of the taxi. John went to help her. When he had finished, he turned to go back to the ferry pier and noticed the black Mercedes G-Wagen idling at the curb at the rear of the taxi rank. He couldn't see inside, the windows were tinted black, but he wasn't about to hang around. He headed for the ferry.

25

FRIDAY

She smiled at him and held out her hand, her eyes sparkling, and his heart leaped as he drank in her beauty. He reached out to take her hand, but his fingers couldn't quite reach. He stretched forward, but for some reason, the gap wouldn't close. He tried harder as a look of alarm filled her face. "John," she cried, and she started receding, her hand moving further from his. A man appeared behind her, his face set in a cruel sneer. He laughed at John, licked his lips, then grabbed her by the hair and pulled her backward. "John, John, help me..." she pleaded. The man dragged her into the darkness. "Wait, Charlotte, wait," John cried out until she disappeared from sight.

John woke with a start, his heart hammering in his chest, the bedsheets soaked. It took a moment for him to realize where he was. He rolled over and looked at his watch on the bedside table. Five a.m. The nightmares were becoming more frequent again. This was the second one this week. He pushed himself up and hung his legs over the side of the bed, leaning forward, his forearms resting on his knees. It had been a long night of fitful sleep. The events of the last few days had raced around in his head, dancing back and forth, his subconscious mind trying to make sense of things. Then in the early hours, once he had finally dropped off to sleep, he had been revisited by his nightmare. There was little point in trying to sleep again, so John resigned himself to a day ahead fueled by coffee.

John rubbed his face and pushed the hair back from his eyes. He padded across to the bathroom and splashed cold water on his face, then walked to the kitchen to make coffee. He needed to be alert and had some serious thinking to do if he was going to get out of this mess.

While the coffee brewed, he turned on his phone, and it buzzed almost immediately with a message. John reluctantly glanced at the screen.

Peter is still alive. It's him or you. Make your choice. You don't have much time left.

John threw the phone onto the kitchen counter and ran his hands through his hair. He had to do something, think of something. If he didn't, he would end up dead himself.

He poured himself a mug of coffee and took a sip as he stared out at the hillside behind the apartment building. He was due to meet Peter at nine a.m., so he had time for a run. He always got his best ideas when he was running, perhaps it would help today.

At the back of his building, a path led straight up the hillside to the ridgeline that ran North to South behind Discovery Bay. It was a steep climb, the path rocky and overgrown, the gradient challenging and guaranteed to make his muscles burn, but the exertion and the pain would clear his mind, it always did. He started slowly, the bruising on his waist and torso hurting with the movement and the deep breathing. It took fifteen minutes to reach the first ridgeline.

He paused to catch his breath, his chest heaving, his legs burning with the lactic acid buildup. The ridge offered panoramic views toward Hong Kong Island in the East, and to the West, the view opened out over the flight path toward Chep Lap Kok Airport, a plane just now making its final approach. The sea breeze dried the sweat from his body, and once he had regained his normal breathing, he set off again, following the ridgeline up toward his destination, Tiger's Head.

At the next false summit, his legs on fire, sweat running down his forehead and stinging his eyes, he stopped and looked around. In the distance, Victoria Peak on Hong Kong Island was shrouded in clouds as were the upper levels of the one-hundred-eighteen-story ICC building across the harbor on the Kowloon reclamation. The long white trail of a ferry's wake curved across the harbor. Closer to hand, a jungle fowl called from the densely forested hillside, and behind him, to the west, another plane made its final approach into Hong Kong airport. John sucked in fresh air and shook the pain out of his calves.

He loved it up here. Just minutes from his home, he was surrounded by nature, not another person to be seen. This was a side of Hong Kong tourists rarely saw and one he loved. He felt calmer now, more at peace, the stress and tension of the last week melting away. Everything was going to be alright. He knew it. A solution would come to him by the time he reached the top of the climb. He took a deep breath, looked up toward the next false summit, and pushed on.

Forty minutes later, he was at the trig point on top of Tiger's Head. Below him, in a three-hundred-sixty-degree arc, lay a magnificent view—the manicured greens of the Discovery Bay Golf Club, and further below, the towers of the various residential communities that made up Discovery Bay. Far off in the mottled green and blue sea lay the islands of Peng Chau, Cheung Chau, and in the distance, the triple smokestacks of the power station on Lamma Island. He could see all the way down to Hong Kong Island, the towers of Central District faintly outlined in the heat haze. The rapidly moving hydrofoil of the Hong Kong Macau Ferry Service crossed paths with the equally rapid Turbojet in the straits below. He turned and looked north to where the one-hundred-fifteen-story tower of Shenzhen's Ping An Finance Centre across the border in China could just be made out.

The breeze at this height was stronger and cooling. Moving from the trig point to the large flat face of a rock, he squatted down, bringing respite to his trembling quads. It was a glorious view, a sight few bothered to climb to enjoy, content instead with roaming the air-conditioned shopping malls down below.

But life was about more than that—John's experiences in India had taught him to value every second, to extract the most out of every day. He had lost his way for a while, his job sucking the life force from his existence, but up here, he felt alive again, filled with the glories of the world. He knew what he had to do now.

Whatever was decided in the meeting with Peter and Joseph this morning, he would take control. It was his life, his destiny, and there was no way he was going to let someone else decide the outcome. Just as he had done before, in that dark time in Bangalore when all had seemed lost, when the one thing he valued most was cruelly taken from him, he would take control and turn things to his advantage. No-one was going to get the better of him. He was going to get himself out of this mess and do all he could to keep the money. That was for sure.

26

J ohn walked up the ferry gangplank and spotted the sleek black S Class Mercedes waiting by the curb. Peter's driver Samuel was standing by the car, looking smart in black pants and a white polo shirt with the Pegasus Land logo embroidered on the front. He smiled at John and waved, opening the rear door as John approached.

"Good morning, sir."

"Good morning, Samuel. How are you?"

"I'm fine, sir. Thank you. Mr. Croft is waiting for you at home."

"Thank you." John slid onto the back seat and settled into the luxurious leather, stretching out his legs, still weary from the early morning climb. A crisp unread copy of that morning's South China Morning Post lay on the armrest next to a chilled bottle of mineral water. John grinned as Samuel walked around to the driver's seat. Life really was better when you had money.

Despite the fitful night's sleep, John felt fresh after his run and a pot of coffee. He sat back and watched the scenery and thought about his situation. Bad luck seemed to have a way of following him around, but he needed to find the silver lining to his cloud. If with Peter's help, he could entrap David Yu, it would solve his immediate problems. However, he wasn't sure he would get to keep the money. The police would probably seize it as evidence so he would have to go back to his shitty job—if they would take him back. It was the last thing he wanted, but he would cross that bridge when he came to it. He had been in worse situations before and had come out on top. He had to let things run their course and make the most out of it.

The car pulled up in front of Peter's entrance, and John stepped out and looked around. The garage doors were open, and John paused for another look at the beautiful Porsches parked inside. One day... if he survived the next few days. He took a deep breath and walked toward the front door.

Imelda opened the door and guided him toward the living room. John stood by the expansive windows, staring out at the view. Thunderclouds were rolling in from the East, bathing the skylines of Hong Kong Island and Kowloon in hues of grey, the top of the ICC tower obscured by clouds.

"Good morning, John."

John turned and smiled at Peter who stood by the kitchen door in workout clothes, his shirt stuck to his chest with sweat, a white hand towel around his neck.

"Good morning, Peter, how are you?"

"Great, nothing beats starting the day with a morning workout. Have you eaten? Come and have some breakfast."

"Thanks, that would be great."

John followed him into the kitchen, and they sat down at the large kitchen island.

Imelda turned and smiled, "Bacon and eggs, sir?"

"Yes, please."

She placed two steaming mugs of black coffee in front of John and Peter and busied herself at the stove.

The smell of frying bacon filled the air, and John looked over at Peter who was checking his phone with a frown. He noticed John watching and clicked off the screen and turned the phone face down on the counter.

"Sorry John, a bad habit, I know."

"Everything alright?"

"Oh yes, just a problem at one of our development sites, but nothing that can't wait. Did you sleep okay?"

"Nothing coffee won't fix."

"Ha, yes, I can't function without the stuff."

Imelda slid a plate of bacon and eggs in front of John.

Peter nodded at the plate, "Enjoy your breakfast. Joseph will be here any moment. We will work out the plans for our meeting tomorrow once you've eaten."

John took a sip of his coffee and picked up his knife and fork.

"John, please excuse me, I'll just make a couple of calls while you're eating. Might as well sort this site issue out now so we can concentrate on our meeting."

"Sure, go ahead."

Peter picked up his phone and his coffee and walked out.

John turned his attention to his plate. The bacon was just how he liked it, still soft and juicy. He hated overcooked bacon. He cut off a piece with his knife and took a bite —superb.

"Thank you, Imelda, it's delicious."

Imelda turned and smiled, her cheeks blushing. "Thank you, sir."

Within minutes, John cleared his plate and downed half

of his coffee. He hadn't realized how hungry he was, the climb up Tiger's Head having built up a huge appetite.

As he sat there dabbing his mouth with a mono-grammed napkin, he felt his phone buzz in his pocket. An all too familiar feeling of dread ran through him as he pulled it out and looked at the screen.

Only two days left. We are watching you.

Suddenly, the bacon didn't taste so good anymore.

27

J ohn pushed back his chair and stood up. He thanked Imelda and walked out into the living room. Peter was nowhere to be seen. John needed some fresh air. Opening the sliding doors onto the pool deck, he stepped out, sliding the door closed behind him. He took a deep breath and exhaled. He couldn't wait until the messages stopped coming. Hopefully, by the end of tomorrow, if all went to plan, his life would be back to normal. He walked over to the edge of the pool deck and looked over the edge. It was a long way down. Once again, he marveled at the engineering needed to support the cantilevered pool. The temperature had dropped, and a strong breeze had whipped up from the east, bringing the threat of rain. The clouds above were dark and ominous, almost as if heralding the looming showdown between him and David Yu.

He looked at his watch... a little after ten a.m., Peter must be ready by now. John just wanted to get the meeting over and done with. He wanted to speed up time and finish things. He turned to look back at the house. Standing in the window, just visible behind the reflected image of the pool deck stood Inspector Joseph Wong, staring at him. It was unnerving, the guy gave him the creeps. Still, he didn't need to be friends with him. He just needed him to arrest David Yu, then he would never have to see him again.

Peter appeared from the back of the room and opened the sliding door.

"John, come on in, Joseph is here. Let's get started."

John walked inside, slid the door shut, and sat on the sofa opposite Peter. Joseph remained standing, just to the right of Peter. He nodded a greeting.

Peter waited while Imelda placed a tray of cups and saucers and a fresh pot of coffee on the table between them.

"That will be all, thank you, Imelda."

Imelda straightened up and smiled. "Yes, sir. I will be in my room if you need me, sir."

Peter waited until she had left the room before speaking.

"John, Joseph and I have come up with a plan we think will work well for all of us. Tomorrow morning, come to my boat at the Aberdeen Marina. I will have Samuel pick you up from the Central Ferry Pier at eleven. It's better you arrive early to avoid any possibility of David or his men spotting you. Joseph will be on the boat already. He will place hidden cameras and recording equipment in the main saloon. We want you to hide in one of the staterooms until David and I arrive at one p.m. You can use the time before then to familiarize yourself with the layout. I will pick David up and bring him to the boat to have lunch and discuss our current project. I'll give him a few glasses of wine, and food will be laid out, so he'll be nice and relaxed."

John nodded and glanced at Joseph who was still staring at him, his eyes unblinking.

Peter continued.

"At two o'clock, you will come out of the stateroom and act as if to kill me. Joseph here will provide you with a weapon." Peter turned toward Joseph who stepped forward, reached behind him, removing a handgun from where it had been tucked inside his waistband. John's eyes widened. He hadn't been expecting a gun.

"What do I need that for?"

"John, we need to make it look realistic. How else do we make it look like you're going through with David's plan?"

John nodded doubtfully. Joseph held out the handgun, and John reached over and took it, feeling the weight in his hand. Holding a weapon made him nervous but also strangely gave him a feeling of power.

Joseph spoke up for the first time. "Have you used one of these before?"

John shook his head.

"It doesn't matter. You just need to point it at Peter. It's loaded, but don't worry about it going off accidentally. It has a passive safety system so nothing will happen unless you pull the trigger. This is a standard issue police weapon, the Glock 17. We just need it for visual effect. Once we have arrested David Yu, I will return it to the weapons store."

John nodded, still feeling doubtful. Things seemed much more serious now that he had a real weapon in his hand.

"Okay. But you still haven't explained how we'll get David to confess."

"That's easy," Peter spoke up. "We'll just present him with the evidence. After we spoke yesterday, I had Joseph pick up the deposit slips from David's office. Joseph also made some inquiries with his contacts inside the triads in Macau. Apparently, David owes a lot of money to a notorious moneylender called Broken Tooth, so we have a motive. I'm also sure once we search David, we will find the phone that has been used to send you the threatening messages."

"But will this be enough to build a case?"

"Don't you worry about that, Mr. Hayes," replied Joseph. "It will be more than enough. Mr. Croft has several friends in the judicial system who will be more than happy to assist. Besides, once I present David Yu with all the evidence and he realizes he is facing a long time in prison, he is sure to co-operate with us. We will make sure David Yu will never bother you or Mr. Croft again."

"But what about me?" asked John. "Nothing will come back on me?"

"John, don't worry, I will look after you. It's obvious you have been acting under duress. I will explain how you have been coerced and also how you have been helping the police and me to make the arrest. You'll be fine," replied Peter.

"Okay," John nodded slowly. His head was full of doubts, he needed time to think them through.

"It will be okay, John," Peter smiled at him. "You have nothing to worry about, we have all the bases covered. I'll make sure you are looked after. You are saving my life, John, and for that, I will be eternally grateful."

John smiled reluctantly. He had no other option but to go along with it.

Peter stood up, shaking Joseph's hand. "Thank you, Joseph." He turned to John. "John, go home, relax. Get a good night's sleep tonight." He reached out and took John's hand in both of his. Looking John straight in the eye, he clasped his hand.

"By tomorrow evening, all this will be over, and we can celebrate together. And John, thank you once again. I owe you my life."

28

John sat deep in thought as he waited for the ferry to depart. He shifted position in his seat, the Glock tucked in his waistband digging into his side, an uncomfortable reminder of the seriousness of his situation. Once the ferry left the pier, John stood up from his seat and walked to the men's toilet at the rear of the deck. Opening the door, he slipped inside and bolted it from the inside. Bracing himself against the rocking of the boat, he removed the gun from his waistband where he had hidden it from sight underneath his untucked shirt and looked at it closely. It was light, weighing not much more than half a kilo, and small. It had been easy to hide under his shirt. He guessed that's why the police used it. It felt good in his hand, but he had no idea how to use it. He flipped the toilet seat down and sat on it.

Resting the weapon on his lap, he pulled out his phone, opened the web browser, and searched for the Glock website. He scrolled through their products until he found the Glock 17, then looked through the specifications. It didn't help him much—there were no instructions on how to use the weapon. He switched to YouTube and grinned. You had to love the internet. There were plenty of videos reviewing the weapon. He looked at his watch—fifteen minutes before the ferry docked in Discovery Bay. Clicking on a video, he started watching. After a six-minute overview of the weapon, he had a fair idea of what to do. He picked up the weapon from his lap and held it in his right hand. With his thumb, he pressed the magazine release lever and ejected the magazine. It popped out onto his lap, and he picked it up. It was empty. John frowned. With his left hand, he pulled back on the slide as he had seen in the video and looked in the chamber. It too was empty. Joseph had given him an unloaded weapon. He supposed it made sense if the idea was just to frighten David, but then why tell him it was loaded? John released the slide, and it slid back into place, cocking the trigger. Satisfied the weapon was empty, John uncocked the trigger, picked up the empty magazine, and slid it back into the weapon. He turned the Glock over and examined the right-hand side. There were two sections that looked like they had been filed away. Someone had filed the serial numbers off—strange. John slid the Glock back into his waistband and pulled his shirt over it. Unlocking the door, he walked back to his seat. Things were definitely not what they seemed. Inspector Joseph Wong was up to something, and John needed to figure out what. John needed a Plan B, a safety net. He picked up his phone and made a call.

29

After freshening up at home, John jumped on the train, took the MTR to Lai King, then changed to the Tsuen Wan Line. From there, he rode the four stops to Sham Shui Po. Sham Shui Po was a notorious working-class area in Kowloon, infamous for its cage homes—squalid apartments that had been subdivided by private landlords into six feet by three feet cages to house the city's poor, sometimes as many as twenty people in an apartment as small as five hundred square feet—ironic in a city that had more Louis Vuitton stores than Paris. The area was also famous for its street food, drawing thousands of visitors from the more affluent areas in the evenings to sample *Chao Tau Fu,* stinky Tofu and bowls of *Hong Tau Sa,* sweet red bean soup. But John wasn't here for that, he had other things on his mind.

He had left the gun at home, hidden under the mattress. He didn't expect anyone to visit his flat while he was away, he just felt more comfortable keeping it out of plain sight. He didn't like guns. The only time he had used one hadn't been pleasant. The thought of what he had done that night back in India sent a shiver up his spine. Steeling himself, he walked through the station to the large map on the wall. He wanted to find the Golden Computer Arcade, an old two-story mall known all over Hong Kong as the place to buy electronics.

He found exit D2 and climbed the steps to street level. He paused and looked around, getting his bearings and breathing in the polluted, humid air. Grimy grey tenements towered above the road, aluminum poles festooned with washing jutted out from the buildings, and ancient air conditioners dripped water on passersby below. Signs advertised karaoke and massage parlors in converted apartments on the upper floors. The streets were packed, crowds of people rushing in both directions, the air filled with the noise of vehicles honking and the sound of multiple languages being spoken at once—Cantonese, Mandarin, Nepali, Urdu.

John grinned as he watched a young Pakistani boy in a full-length kaftan run down the street, followed by his little sister in a headscarf. He had hated his job, but he loved the city. It had a buzz like no other, an energy that soaked through your pores and became addictive. Everywhere you looked, it was full of contrasts. This area couldn't be further removed from the glitzy world of luxury mansions and exotic cars David Yu inhabited, yet it was just a short train ride across the harbor. John was sure neither David nor Peter had ever stepped foot in this place.

The thought of them reminded him why he was there. He glanced behind him, looking for a tail, but in these crowds, it was impossible to spot anyone who shouldn't be there. He hadn't noticed anyone on the train so would have to take his chances.

John waited for a taxi to pass, then crossed the road to

the Golden Computer Arcade. The arcade was on two levels, the ground floor and basement of a residential building. He climbed the short flight of steps from the street and pushed his way through the crowd, wandering along the aisles, studying the shops for the one he wanted. Small shops overflowing with computer and gaming equipment, pirated software, and cut-price laptops lined each side, every shop full with customers of all ages

Spotting a shop that looked suitable, John wandered in and scanned the shelves. A salesman wandered over, a young man with a ready smile, and asked John in English if he needed any help. John explained what he was looking for, but the man didn't stock it. He suggested another store a few doors down. Sure enough, the shop had what John wanted, an item which was surprisingly easily available, and John made the purchase and left.

His stomach growled as he left the mall, and he realized he hadn't eaten anything since breakfast. Once out on the street, he turned left and walked toward Fuk Wa Street. He was really hungry and spotted the New Kashmir Halal Restaurant on the next street. There were some things he didn't miss about his time in India, but food wasn't one of them. Pushing the door open, he walked inside. A table of Pakistani and Nepali youths eyed him suspiciously, but he walked past and took a table at the back, facing the door. He ordered a plate of Mutton curry and garlic naan, watching the street while he waited. Crowds of people streamed past the door, and he watched them without paying much attention until, through a momentary gap in the crowd, he thought he saw a man in black watching the restaurant from the other side of the street. He narrowed his eyes and concentrated, trying to get a better look, but he couldn't see him again. He must be getting paranoid.

After he finished, he walked outside, his taste buds craving something sweet after the spice-laden food. Immediately next door, a shop sold tofu in a sweet soup and was packed with customers with more queuing up to be seated, but he had never been a big fan of tofu. He headed back to the MTR station and spotted a stall selling sweets made of rice and sugar. He bought a sticky rice flour bun, filled with sweetened red bean. Turning, he faced the street while he ate the dessert. Again, he thought he saw a man in black watching him, but then lost him in the crowd. John shrugged. There was nothing more he could do. He had one more purchase to make, then he would head home.

30

J ohn leaned back against the headrest as the Mercedes wound its way through Pok Fu Lam, along the north-western edge of Hong Kong Island. Samuel had been there to pick him up from the ferry as arranged the previous day.

John's nerves were jumping—he had slept badly and had needed a lot of coffee to get him started. Now the caffeine was increasing his anxiety as the car approached Aberdeen Marina. The gun was inside a large zip-lock bag which John had tucked into his waistband, under his shirt. He had given it a thorough wipe down the previous evening, removing all his fingerprints from the weapon, then carefully placed it inside the bag.

Peter had assured him he would be alright, but for some reason John couldn't put his finger on, he didn't trust the cop. The guy gave him the creeps, the way he was always watching him. John was suspicious now he had provided him with an unloaded weapon despite saying it was loaded. So, John had a plan of his own in mind, a card up his sleeve. Hopefully, he wouldn't need to play it, but it was there in reserve if needed. John closed his eyes and deepened his breathing in an attempt to relax. He had done everything he could that was in his control. He had to go with the flow now and hope everything worked out.

The Mercedes slowed as it approached the Marina Club, then turned right and pulled to a stop in front of the entrance gate to the yacht berths.

"Here we are, sir." Samuel turned in his seat and smiled back at John.

"Thank you, Samuel." John inhaled deeply, paused for a moment, then opened the door. He stepped out into the heat, making sure his shirt remained over the gun in his waistband and straightened up. He looked around, but the street was empty, there was no one around. John walked to the security gate, entered the passcode Peter had texted him earlier into the keypad and stepped inside. Peter's boat, being one of the larger boats in the marina, was on one of the farthest berths. John followed the path around in front of the Marina Club and past the pier for the Jumbo Floating Restaurant. The boats increased in size as he moved further from the entrance, and by the time he reached the last pontoon, the boats ranged from sixty to a hundred feet in length. Peter's boat was at the end, and as John neared, his mouth fell open.

He had suspected Peter had a large boat, but this was huge. It stretched from one end of the pontoon to the other, a sleek, black-hulled Azimut at least one hundred feet in length. John knew nothing about boats, but this was beautiful. An inflatable tender was tied to the swim deck at the rear, and on the stern of the boat, the name Pegasus was written in large chrome letters. Above that, the flag of the British Virgin Islands waved gently in the breeze. A pile of shoes lay on the wooden pontoon, so taking his cue, John removed his and stepped onto the boat. He climbed the steps that led from the swimming platform onto the aft deck just as the rear door slid open, and Inspector Joseph walked out.

"Good morning," John greeted him

Joseph nodded at him.

"Come inside." He turned and walked back in. John shook his head. Joseph would never win Miss Congeniality.

John followed him inside, slid the door closed behind him, and turned, looking around. He knew the yacht was big, but the space inside was unbelievable. A huge saloon with L shaped sofas upholstered in soft cream leather and adorned with scatter cushions. Behind the seating area was an eight-seat dining table, already set up with place settings for two. On the other side of the dining area, at the forward part of the deck, was a luxuriously appointed galley which would be the envy of many a homeowner. To the right of the galley, a staircase led up to the bridge, and to the left, a set of stairs led down to the lower deck. On this deck alone, the space was more than John had in his entire apartment.

Joseph stood by the dining table, watching him look around and cleared his throat impatiently.

"John, Peter and Mr. Yu will sit here for lunch." He indicated the chair with its back to the stairs. "Mr. Yu will sit here. Peter will sit over there, opposite Mr. Yu."

"Okay."

"I've set up hidden cameras and microphones to record everything."

John nodded and looked around. He couldn't see anything. "Where are they?"

"It's better you don't know. Otherwise, you will be conscious of them, and it won't look genuine. We want it to appear as natural as possible, so Mr. Yu doesn't get spooked."

"Will there be anyone else on the boat? What about serving staff or crew?"

"Peter wanted it kept to the minimum for safety. He didn't want any of his staff harmed unnecessarily, just in case anything goes wrong, so he has given them all the day off."

John frowned. "What could go wrong?"

"We are just playing it safe. Don't worry. The caterers will deliver the lunch at twelve-thirty, then leave. Clear?"

"How about your colleagues?"

"There is no need, I can handle Mr. Yu by myself. Don't worry. Just do everything as we have planned, and there will be no problems. Clear?"

John nodded.

"Good. Now follow me." Joseph headed down the stairs to the lower deck. John followed him but paused beside the dining table and removed the small listening device he had bought in Sham Shui Po from his pocket, quickly sticking it to the underside of the table, away from sight. It was voice activated and contained a telephone SIM. Any conversations would be recorded and saved as files in the cloud which John could access later. Satisfied it wouldn't be seen, he followed Joseph down the stairs, and they stepped into a narrow corridor. Joseph walked to the rear, opened the door into the master suite, and walked inside.

"This is where you will hide until about one thirty. Then you come up the stairs and confront Peter with the gun. Once Mr. Yu sees you, I want you to turn the gun on him. You have the gun?"

John nodded.

"Good. Be very careful with it. We can't afford for anyone

to get hurt. I will join you, and we will all confront Mr. Yu and force a confession out of him."

John frowned. It didn't really seem like a great plan, and again, Joseph was referring to the weapon being loaded. It was all very strange, but he hoped it would work as they had no other options.

"So, now I wait?"

"Yes. I'm going up to check on the equipment once again, then I'll come down and hide in one of the other rooms just before one o'clock."

John nodded. "Okay." He looked at his watch—almost twelve. He had an hour before things got underway. He may as well make himself comfortable. Joseph let himself out, closing the door behind him.

John looked around the spacious master suite. The room took up the entire width of the boat with a king-sized bed in the center of the room, and as on the upper deck, padded cream leather lined the walls. A white, lacquered writing desk took up the space underneath the full-length windows on the port side, and a coffee table and two easy chairs sat under the window on the starboard side. On either side of the bedhead, two doors led into an en-suite bathroom. John reached into his pocket and removed the pair of latex gloves he had bought the day before and slipped them on before opening the en-suite door and poking his head inside.

A polished, white marble countertop above shiny, white lacquer cabinets gleamed in the light from the multiple spotlights overhead. The port side of the bathroom contained a full-size bath and washbasin, and the starboard side held the WC and another washbasin. Separating the two was a glass and timber-paneled sauna. The bathroom was much bigger than the one in his apartment and certainly more luxurious. Not for the first time, John realized he had chosen the wrong career path.

John glanced up at his reflection in the full-height mirror—his forehead was creased in a frown, and dark smudges under his eyes were proof of the strain he had been under in the past week. He was looking forward to this being over.

He walked back out into the bedroom and paused by the windows which stretched the length of the room. The windows were tinted, so he had no concerns about being spotted from the dock. He walked over to the seaward side of the boat and gazed out at the view. The sea appeared to be just below the window, and in the near distance, he could see anchored out in the channel the large floating Jumbo Seafood Restaurant, starting to fill up with customers for lunch. A heavily laden sampan passed the Pegasus as it ferried customers to the restaurant while an empty boat headed back for its next load. The sun shone down brightly from the clear blue sky above. It would have been an ideal day to spend on a boat—if only the circumstances had been different. John sighed and turned back to the bed.

May as well get some rest before the main event. He laid back on the bed and closed his eyes. Nothing to do now but wait.

31

At around twelve-thirty, John heard a noise outside on the dock and opened his eyes. He slid off the bed and cracked the door open. The sound of voices and movement upstairs carried down to him as the caterers delivered the food. He wanted to stretch his legs, so he pulled the door open wide and stepped out into the corridor. The corridor led past the stairs toward the front of the boat with a door to each side and another door at the front. John walked forward carefully, conscious not to make any noise and checked each room. The door to the right opened onto a stateroom with two single berths and to the left another double berth stateroom. At the end of the corridor, in the bow, a door opened onto one more double berthed stateroom which, like the other two rooms, was empty but had a sports bag lying on the bed. John looked behind him to make sure he wasn't being observed, then stepped inside, closing the door behind him. He crossed to the bed and unzipped the bag. Inside was a bundle of plastic zip ties, a cell phone, and another Glock in a holster. John picked up the Glock, removed it from the holster, and pressed the button to release the magazine. It was loaded. John reached behind him and removed the zip-lock bag containing the Glock and carefully opened it, removing the weapon and laying it on the bed. He put the zip-lock bag in his pocket, then popped the empty magazine from his Glock and replaced it with the loaded one from the bag. With care, and remembering what he had learned the previous day, he pulled back the slide on Joseph's Glock and ejected the live round from the chamber. He released the slide, then pulled it back again to double check the chamber was empty before slotting in the empty magazine from his own Glock. He slid it back into the holster and placed it back in the kitbag. He picked up the live round from the bed and slipped it into his pocket, zipping the bag shut. He hoped he wouldn't have to use it but felt better knowing he was the one with the loaded weapon. He looked at his watch. Not long to go now. Tucking the Glock back into his waistband, he moved back to the master suite, taking care to keep to the side away from the stairs, in case anyone was looking down, and let himself back into the suite. Unable to relax, he stood by the window, watching the boat traffic, and tried not to think of what was to come.

Just after one p.m., he again heard voices and felt the boat shift as someone came onboard. John looked at his watch. That must be Peter and David. His heart rate increased, and his forehead started to perspire. He stiffened as he heard someone coming down the stairs. Slipping inside the en-suite bathroom, he pulled the door closed. The door to the master bedroom opened, and John tensed.

A voice whispered, "John, are you in here?"

Peter.

John opened the door and looked out. Peter had tucked

his head in and grinned when he saw John. He gave him a thumbs up.

"All set?" he whispered.

John nodded and returned the thumbs up. Peter glanced at his gloved hands, a shadow passing across his face briefly, but then he nodded, smiled, and closed the door. There was no sign of Joseph, but John assumed he was hiding in one of the other cabins.

John went back into the en-suite, grabbed a mono-grammed hand towel and wiped down any surfaces he may have touched. He had a gnawing feeling in his gut he had to look after himself, and this seemed to be the right thing to do. It never paid to trust too many people. When he was done, he removed the Glock from his waistband and sat at the foot of the bed, facing the door and waited.

32

J ohn had cracked open the door so he could hear what was happening, and the voices from the deck above had become louder in the last thirty minutes. He couldn't make out the words, but the tone seemed happy enough. He heard the pop of a champagne cork and the clinking of glasses, followed by laughter and what seemed like a friendly discussion. Once he heard the clatter of cutlery on plates, he stood up and took a couple of deep breaths. He looked down at his shaking hands and felt nauseous. He took another deep breath. It was time to put an end to this. Then he would lie on a beach, somewhere quiet, and do nothing.

He opened the door wider and stepped out. There was still no sign of Joseph. The front stateroom door was closed, and John assumed he was in there. He hoped Joseph hadn't checked his weapon. John felt safer having the loaded weapon—he didn't trust Joseph at all. He was sure Joseph had an ulterior motive but wasn't sure what it was yet.

John padded softly to the bottom of the stairs and looked up. He couldn't see anyone but could now hear the conversation clearly and paused to listen in. He could hear Peter's voice.

"David, we need to push ahead on the reclamation bid. Without that contract, we won't get the government subsidies we are seeking."

"Peter, I'm not sure. I've said this before, we are stretching ourselves too thin." He hesitated, then continued, "Father says we should consolidate the projects we have already. Take things easy and pay down the debts, instead of constantly expanding."

"Come on, David," Peter exhaled loudly. "Stop listening to your father. You are a successful businessman yourself. You can make your own decisions."

"Yes but…"

"I don't understand why you are being so cautious. If it wasn't for me pushing things forward, we wouldn't have grown the company to the size it is. We need to keep growing, we need to keep expanding."

"Peter, I appreciate everything you have done, and I respect the efforts you have made in making the company what it is today. But this constant expansion has stretched the company's finances to the max. We are spending more than we are making. Even this boat. Do we really need it? We shouldn't have bought it."

Peter's voice became more forceful, frustration evident in his tone. "I told you at the time, it would be a valuable asset for the company. We entertain clients on it, and it projects a successful image to our suppliers and financiers. Why are we having this discussion again?"

"I just…" David's voice trailed off. John strained to hear him. "I just feel it's unnecessary. We have payments due this quarter which we will not make if we bid on the reclamation. We have to consolidate."

John frowned as he listened. There seemed to be more going on than he first thought. Is this why David wanted Peter dead? He wanted to slow down the expansion, pare down debts, and siphon off cash to pay his gambling debts? Or was there more going on? David didn't sound unreasonable.

He heard a door click behind him and quickly turned. Joseph was standing in the corridor, a tense expression on his face. He had his weapon in one hand, a handful of cable ties in the other and gestured for John to hurry and climb the stairs. John nodded, took a deep breath, and climbed. As his head cleared the deck above, he could see David sitting with his back to him, Peter across from him. Peter could see John but ignored him, keeping his focus on David. John climbed higher, raising the gun and pointing it at Peter as he stepped onto the deck. Peter turned to look at him, and his eyes went wide in feigned horror. He pushed back his chair and raised his hands in the air.

"What the...?"

David swiveled around, and his mouth dropped open at the sight of John pointing his gun at Peter. His cutlery clattered onto the table, and he shoved his chair backward, scrambling to get out of the way, the napkin falling off his lap onto the floor. As he backed up against the side of the boat, he raised his hands, looking from John to Peter in a panic.

"Wh... wh... what's going on?" he stammered.

John turned and pointed the gun at David.

"No, no, what do you want?" David cried out as he cowered against the side of the boat, a wet patch appearing on the front of his pants.

Peter grinned and lowered his hands.

"You thought you would get away with this, David. Hire

someone to kill me, then take over the company. Well, I'm smarter than you. We found out what you had planned. John here has been helping me. You are going to prison for a very long time."

"What?" David looked from Peter to John and back again, the puzzlement evident on his face. "What are you saying?" He turned to John, "Broken Tooth didn't send you?"

John frowned. "Who?"

"Broken Tooth. I owe him money."

"No. You sent me to kill Peter. You have been threatening me. On the phone."

"What? Who are you?" David shook his head, confusion clearly written across his face. He looked from John to Peter and back again. "Why would I threaten you? I don't even know who you are."

John frowned. David looked like he was telling the truth, but Peter seemed genuine too. What the hell was going on? He hesitated and lowered the gun slightly. He glanced over at Peter who was frowning at David.

"Peter, what is going on here?"

Peter turned to face John. He opened his mouth to speak, and at the same time, his eyes flicked over John's shoulder. Too late, John sensed a movement behind him, then a blinding pain in the back of his head, followed by darkness.

33

John opened his eyes. He was face down on the carpet, and his head was throbbing. He tried to move his arms to push himself up, but they appeared to be fastened behind him. He rolled onto his side and pulled his knees up to his chest before swinging his legs around in front and pushing himself against the wall behind him. Using his legs and the wall for leverage, he maneuvered himself up into a seated position. Directly in front of him, leaning against the wall on the other side of the cabin was David, his arms bound behind him, his feet secured with plastic cable ties. He watched John as he sat up. John looked around the cabin—they were alone—then looked back at David. He looked scared, his hair ruffled, and his pants still wet where he had peed himself.

"What happened?"

"Someone hit you from behind, then he and Peter made me drag you down here before tying us up."

"Shit. What's going on?"

"You're sure you weren't sent by Broken Tooth?"

"Who the fuck is Broken Tooth?"

"I owe him a lot of money. He's the *Shan Tsiu*. You know what that means?"

"No."

"It means Mountain Master. He is the leader of the biggest triad in Macau, the 14K."

"But you've been texting me. You put a million dollars in my account, then threatened me, told me I had to kill Peter, or you would kill me."

"What?" David shook his head. "Why would I put a million dollars in your account? I don't even know who you are. You've been following me. I saw you in the Captain's Bar. I got an anonymous call telling me Broken Tooth had employed a *gweilo* to kill me. You."

John frowned and leaned his head back against the wall and closed his eyes. He needed to think. The whole situation was very confusing. He didn't understand what was going on, and things were getting more complicated by the minute. He opened his eyes again and looked across at David.

"So, you had nothing to do with the messages I've been getting?"

David shook his head.

"And you know absolutely nothing about me?"

"No."

John narrowed his eyes. It was evident Peter was not the friend he had made himself out to be. They needed to get off the boat. John moved his arms and flexed his wrists. They were bound tightly with plastic cable ties as were his feet. He looked around the cabin. If he could find a blade or some other sharp object, maybe he could stand back to back with David, and they could cut each other's hand restraints.

John bent his legs and pulled his feet toward him, leaning forward until his bodyweight was over his feet.

"What are you doing?" David asked.

"Getting us out of here." John grunted with effort as he pushed himself to his feet. He wobbled as he stood up but with effort, regained his balance. David looked up at him, fear and puzzlement struggling for prominence on his face. John hopped toward the door and pressed his ear to the door's surface, listening carefully. He could just make out voices and the sound of movement coming from the upper deck. There were still people onboard. He had to move fast. He turned and looked around the cabin again. His eyes landed on the writing desk, and he hopped over toward it. The surface of the desk was devoid of any items, so he turned his attention to the drawers. Turning his back to the desk, he leaned back toward it and with his fingers, pulled the left-hand drawer open. He twisted around and looked inside. Just paper and a few pens and pencils. He hopped over to the right-hand side and repeated the maneuver with the right-hand drawer. A small pair of scissors lay in the drawer. That would do. He turned, leaned back and scrabbled with his fingertips until he felt the scissors, then picked them up. He looked over at David's anxious face and grinned.

John hopped across the cabin until he was in front of David.

"You need to stand up. I'm getting us out of here."

David pulled his feet underneath him and tried to stand. He was much heavier than John, and by the state of his physique, didn't look like he ever did much exercise. He struggled but couldn't stand up.

"Come on, man. Put some effort into. If we stay here, they will kill us."

David looked up in shock, then redoubled his efforts.

"Push your back against the wall, use it as leverage."

With great strain, he finally raised himself off the floor and stood up, his chest heaving with the effort, his forehead glistening with sweat.

"Good, now turn around, so your back is toward me."

David hopped around until he faced away from John. John hopped closer and moved, so his back was facing David's, then opened the scissors with the fingers of his right hand. He leaned back toward David until their hands were touching, then positioned the scissor blades, so they were pointing upwards and slid them over the cable ties. He closed the scissors as much as he could with his fingers and tried to cut the cable tie, but the angle made the movement difficult, and he couldn't close them enough.

"Bugger it." He tried again, but the blades kept slipping over the cable tie and not cutting. This would take longer than he thought. With considerable difficulty, he slid the blade of the scissors up and down along the edge of the cable tie, trying to cut a groove in the plastic. His fingers ached with the effort, and his shoulders were cramping. He gritted his teeth—it was painful, but he had to keep going. They had to get free before Peter or Joseph came downstairs. He stopped for a moment, rolling his shoulders, easing the cramp, then started again.

"Is it working?" David asked.

"I don't know," John sighed, "but it's the only idea I have right now." A movement in the corner of his eye caught his attention, and he looked to his left out the window. He grinned. Everything would be okay. Thank goodness for Plan B.

34

Thapa lowered his binoculars and looked at his watch. It had been an hour and a half since David Yu had boarded the yacht. According to the plan John had discussed with Thapa over the phone, the police should have arrested David Yu by now and escorted him off the boat. There was no sign of the police and no sign of John. It was time for Thapa to move in and put John's backup plan into play. He nodded to the man standing next to him.

"*Garaum,* Let's go."

Tejpal Bahadur Rai rolled his shoulders back, cricked his neck to the left and the right, then grinned at his son. It had been many years since he had seen any action, and he was raring to go.

Father and son climbed down from the jetty where they had been observing the Pegasus and into the inflatable boat moored at the side. Thapa twisted the throttle handle and pulled the starter cord twice until the engine fired up. His father untied the lines, and they headed slowly across the marina toward the Pegasus.

Thapa guided the boat past as if heading out into the channel, then turned the boat back toward the Pegasus. He killed the engine and allowed momentum to carry them toward the large yacht. Thapa concentrated on guiding the inflatable toward the bow of the Pegasus, and the inflatable gently bumped up against the hull of the boat. Tejpal stood up, bracing himself against the hull. Thapa stood beside him, careful not to rock the boat, then boosted his father until he could catch the lip of the deck and pulled himself up easily. Tejpal prided himself on keeping fit and had the strength and agility of a man half his age. Thapa threw a line up, and Tejpal secured the inflatable to the railing, then reached down for Thapa's hand and helped him onboard. Both men squatted in the bow.

Tejpal removed the backpack from his back and reached inside, pulling out a large curved leather sheath. He looked at Thapa and winked. Holding the sheath in his left hand, with his right he removed a highly polished curved blade, the deadly khukuri the Gurkhas were feared all around the world for. Thapa nodded and grinned. He raised his head to look over the side on the land side of the boat. All clear. Thapa turned to his father and nodded.

"*Ahile*, Now."

Thapa waved his father forward, down the port side of the boat while he advanced down the starboard side, keeping a low profile, bent at the waist. He reached a side door that opened into the main saloon and crouched down. He took a deep breath, counted to three, then straightened up and opened the door.

Two men stood inside, deep in conversation—a fit looking Chinese man in cargo pants and a loose shirt, and a middle-aged *gweilo*. Thapa didn't know who the Chinese man was but assumed by the way the *gweilo* was dressed, and his deep tan he was Peter Croft. Both men looked at him in alarm.

"Who are you?" the Chinese man demanded. At that moment, a door on the other side of the saloon opened, and Tejpal stepped inside, the gleaming blade of his khukuri glinting in his right hand. Both men swiveled to look in his direction, and the Chinese man reached behind him and removed a handgun from his waistband. He stepped back, pulling Peter back with him with his left hand. He raised the weapon and pointed it first at Tejpal and then Thapa. "I said, who are you?"

Thapa raised his hands. "Where's John?" he asked. Tejpal hefted the khukuri in his hand and scowled.

The Chinese man's eyes widening, he glanced at Peter. "John who?"

"We saw him come on the boat. Where is he?"

"I don't know who John is, but you need to get off this boat now. You are trespassing."

Peter edged behind the Chinese man and backed toward the door at the rear of the saloon.

"John?" Thapa called out. There was no reply.

"Thapa." Tejpal glanced in his direction before fixing his eyes back on the man with the gun. "*Tala jamca garnuhos,* Check below."

Thapa, his hands still raised in the air, stepped back slowly toward the stairs.

"Stay where you are!" the Chinese man screamed, pointing the weapon back at Thapa. Thapa tensed, spread his feet, a slight bend in his knees, ready to move at any moment. He glanced across at his father, poised like a cat ready to pounce, his khukuri raised in his right hand. Without taking his eyes off the gun, his father gave a slight nod.

"*Jao*, go."

Thapa leaped for the stairs. The Chinese man pulled the trigger. Click. Nothing happened. He looked down at the gun in horror. He pulled the trigger again. Click. Click.

With a blood-curdling cry, "*Ayo Gorkhali!*" Tejpal rushed forward, his khukuri raised above his head. The Chinese man froze in terror, his mouth hanging open in shock. Tejpal brought the blade down, at the last minute changing the angle, striking the Chinese man on the side of the head with the flat of the blade, knocking him to the ground. He kicked him in the stomach, knocking all the air out of him and kicked the Glock out of his reach. He then sat on top of him, holding the blade of the khukuri to his throat.

"Move, and I will kill you," he growled.

"Papa?" Thapa called out from the stairs.

"*Ma thika chu.* I'm okay."

Thapa ran down the stairs and looked around.

"John?" he called out.

"In here," came the muffled reply.

Thapa turned and moved to the door at the stern end of the boat. He opened it and looked inside at John standing with his back to a plump middle-aged Chinese man who appeared to have wet his pants.

Thapa grinned. "Need some help?"

35

J ohn grinned back. "Did you bring coffee?"

Thapa walked over and took the scissors from John's hand and cut him loose, then bent down and cut the cable ties securing John's feet. John rotated his wrists and stepped side to side, getting the blood flowing again.

"What about this guy?" Thapa asked with a jerk of his head at David cowering against the side of the boat.

"Cut his feet loose but leave his hands. I need to ask him some questions. Was there anyone on board?"

"A *gweilo* and a Chinese guy. My father has secured the Chinese guy."

"Joseph. What about Peter?"

"The *gweilo*? I don't know."

"Okay, let's take this guy upstairs and decide what to do."

Thapa grabbed David by the arm and shoved him out the door. John followed him out, and as Thapa pushed David up the stairs, John went to the forward cabin. Joseph's kit bag was still lying on the bed, and John removed a handful of cable ties before heading upstairs.

Thapa waited for John in the galley, a terrified-looking David by his side.

"Make him sit over there," John indicated toward the sofa in the saloon with a jerk of his head. Thapa pushed him down into the sofa, then turned to John.

"John, this is my father."

John looked toward the rear of the saloon where a powerful-looking man sat astride Joseph.

"Mr. Rai, a pleasure to meet you. And thank you."

Tejpal grinned back.

"What happened to the other guy?"

Tejpal nodded toward the open rear door. "I'm sorry John, but he got away."

John walked to the back and stepped out the door. He looked around, but there was no sign of Peter anywhere, and the tender was missing from the rear of the boat.

"Shit."

He stepped back inside and looked down at Joseph who was scowling back at him despite having a wicked-looking blade held to his throat. John passed Tejpal the cable ties.

"Use these. We need to question him."

Tejpal rolled Joseph over and bound his hands together, then pulled Joseph to his feet and shoved him toward the sofa where he forced him to sit next to David. David shifted away from him, trying to keep as much distance as possible.

Joseph sneered at the men standing in front of him.

"You are in big trouble. I am a police officer. I will see that you spend the rest of your lives in prison."

John walked over to the dining table and removed the listening device from underneath, holding it up for Joseph to see.

"Maybe we should listen to what's on this?"

Joseph's face changed, his look of defiance faltering.

"Yes, I thought so." John pursed his lips. "It would seem Peter has not been as honest with me as I thought."

He looked at Tejpal. "Mr. Rai, please take him downstairs. Secure him in one of the cabins. We'll question him later." Tejpal nodded and pulled Joseph off the sofa and shoved him toward the stairs. Joseph sniggered at John and spat on the floor in front of him.

John ignored Joseph and grabbed a chair from the dining area, placed it in front of David, and sat down. Thapa perched on the arm of the opposite sofa.

"David, perhaps we should start with you."

"I don't know anything," David sniveled. "I thought you worked for Broken Tooth."

"So, you haven't been texting me?"

"No," David shook his head violently. "I don't even know who you are."

"You didn't put a million dollars in my account?"

"Why would I do that?"

"Because you owe money, and you wanted me to kill Peter so you could take control of Pegasus and sell off the assets to pay your debts."

David stared at John in disbelief, his mouth hanging open. He shook his head slowly and looked from John to Thapa and back again.

"Yes, I owe money, but I would never kill Peter. I'm not a criminal."

John studied his face for a moment. His protestations sounded genuine, and he appeared to be genuinely scared.

"I found deposit slips in your office at Pegasus Land. One million dollars paid into my account in cash."

David shook his head in disbelief. "I haven't been to that office in weeks. I have other businesses to run. I talk to Peter on the phone, but I hardly ever go to the office."

John frowned and thought for a moment, trying to make things add up. But the more he thought, the more confusing things seemed.

"Why did you have me beaten up?"

"What? When?"

"Earlier this week. Two tattooed thugs in a black G-Wagen."

A look of recognition dawned on David's face.

"Father." David looked up at John. "Where were you?"

"I was following you from your house."

David nodded. "My father likes to keep an eye on me, unfortunately. Look, I don't know what has been going on, but I promise you, I have had nothing to do with any messages or money in your account."

"Okay," John nodded slowly. "Maybe I believe you. But one thing I don't understand. You are rich. Why would you borrow money from a guy called Broken Tooth?"

David sighed. "You don't know my father." He cast his eyes down to the floor. He looked up again and stared earnestly at John. "I've never been good enough for him. He watches over everything I do." He shook his head. "I'm forty years old... he still has me on an allowance, for God's sake." His shoulders slumped as he looked down at his feet again. "My cars and the casinos are my only escape." He sighed again. "But I've had some bad luck," he looked up at John, "and I can't tell my father. He will kill me."

John stood up and paced around the saloon. Thapa watched him as David slumped back into the sofa, his body language defeated. John paused and looked out the window —at the boats passing in the channel, the garish multicolored hulk of the Jumbo floating restaurant. He came to a decision. He turned back and looked at Thapa.

"Cut him loose but watch over him while I search the boat."

He nodded at Tejpal who was standing at the top of the stairs, his khukuri ever present in his right hand.

"Mr. Rai, perhaps you can help me?"

Tejpal nodded and passed the khukuri to Thapa. John followed him downstairs. They started at the front cabin and searched the cupboards but found nothing. John picked up Joseph's bag and searched it again. There was no sign of any recording equipment, just more cable ties, the empty gun holster, and a change of clothes.

The other cabins turned up nothing of interest, so they moved to the rear cabin where Joseph laid, bound hand and foot on the floor.

"*Tiu lei lo mo*. Motherfucker. You will never get away with this," he sneered. John kicked him in the groin as he walked past which put a quick end to any conversation.

The cupboards only contained Peter's clothing, so John moved to the writing desk. The drawers he had searched before, but below the drawers was a locked door. He searched through the drawers again for a key but couldn't find anything.

"Mr. Rai, see if you can find anything we can use to open this."

Tejpal nodded and left the room. John continued searching the bathroom cabinets and under the bed but found nothing. Tejpal appeared in the doorway with his khukuri and a grin.

"Try this, John."

John took it from him and hefted the blade in his hand, admiring the craftsmanship. It must have weighed about half a kilo and was approximately forty centimeters long. The blade curved in a semi-circle away from the polished wood handle, the cutting-edge concave. On one side was engraved the Gurkha war cry "*Ayo Gorhkali*, The Gurkhas are here."

It was an impressive weapon, and John was reluctant to use it for something so mundane as opening a cupboard. He looked back at Tejpal.

"Are you sure?"

Tejpal nodded.

John turned and slid the blade between the edge of the door and the desk. He levered the door outwards, and the wood around the lock splintered and gave way. He passed the khukuri back to Tejpal and bent down to look inside... and whistled. Reaching inside, he pulled out a brick of five-hundred-dollar notes bound with a rubber band and tossed them on the bed. There were more inside, and he pulled them all out until there was a pile on the bed. John stood up and winked at Tejpal.

"I think we'll need a bag."

36

Tejpal and John rejoined Thapa upstairs after locking the main cabin door with Joseph inside. They weren't sure what to do with him, so they put the decision off until later.

"Let's go. I need to listen to the recording and try to work out what has been going on."

"What about him?" Thapa nodded at David sitting on the sofa.

"Bring him with us. I'm inclined to believe him, but until I sort this out, let's hang on to him."

Tejpal retrieved his backpack from the bow of the boat and came back inside, removing the leather sheath from the bag. With the khukuri, he made a small cut on his thumb, drawing blood, then slid the blade inside its sheath. He noticed John watching.

"Tradition," he replied to John's unspoken question with a smile.

John looked around the saloon, making sure he wasn't leaving anything behind. He spied the Glock lying on the kitchen benchtop. He picked it up, realizing he was still wearing the latex gloves. He popped the magazine and found it was the loaded one. He slid the magazine back in and handed it to Tejpal.

"Here, this might be useful. Careful, it's loaded." Tejpal took it with the familiarity of an ex-army man and tucked it into his waistband.

John noticed for the first time a sports jacket draped over the dining chair Peter had occupied earlier. He walked over and searched the pockets. He found a set of house keys, Peter's wallet, and an iPhone. The phone was locked, he would have to deal with it later. He stowed it in Joseph's kit bag, along with the keys and the wallet.

"Let's go."

Thapa helped David to his feet and pushed him toward the rear door.

As John neared the rear door, he spotted Joseph's Glock lying on the floor. He bent over and picked it up, and as he walked out onto the rear deck, tossed it over the side. He slid the rear door of the saloon closed behind him and removed the latex gloves, tucking them into his pocket. Looking around, he sucked in a deep breath of air. The sky was clear, not a cloud to be seen, and the water sparkled in the light of the sun. He was happy to be alive.

37

J ohn, Tejpal, and David took the long walk back along the pontoons to the shore while Thapa retrieved the borrowed inflatable from the bow of the Pegasus.

He was already at the dock by the time they arrived, then the four of them walked out the gate onto the road.

"My car is over there, John," said Thapa, waving at a silver mini-van parked across the road.

They crossed the road, and Thapa unlocked the vehicle with a blip of his key-fob. He was about to open the door when a black Mercedes G-Wagen pulled up beside them, all four doors opening and four hard-looking men got out and encircled them.

"Shit," John cursed

Tejpal and Thapa tensed beside him, Tejpal reaching behind him for the Glock tucked into his waistband.

A sleek, black 1960s Rolls Royce Silver Cloud purred to a stop behind the Mercedes, the view inside hidden by curtained windows.

David's shoulders slumped even more. "Father."

One of the thugs walked back to the Rolls Royce and opened the door, beckoning to David. David sighed.

"Wait here, I'll speak to him." He walked over, bent down and looked inside. A conversation ensued, but John couldn't understand what was said. Instead, he kept his eyes on the men surrounding him. Eventually, David turned back to John.

"He wants to speak to you."

John looked at Thapa and Tejpal.

"It's okay, they won't be harmed," David reassured him.

John nodded and handed the kitbag to Thapa. "Here take care of this."

Thapa nodded, keeping his eyes on the men lined up around them. John walked over to the Rolls Royce and looked inside at the elderly Chinese man dressed in a dark suit, his white shirt buttoned up to the collar but no tie. His hands rested on a black cane with a silver dragon on the handle.

"Mr. Hayes, you are a very resourceful man."

"Mr. Yu."

"Perhaps you would like to take a ride with me, Mr. Hayes? I think we have a lot to discuss."

"How can I trust you?"

"I can assure you, Mr. Hayes, I will not harm you. You have my word. You have a bigger enemy to worry about. Your men will be safe too. Tell them they can go."

John looked at Ronald Yu, weighing his decision, then straightened up, turning back to Thapa and Tejpal.

"It's okay. Go home. I will call you later."

"Are you sure, John?"

"Yes, Thapa. I'll call you... and thank you."

Thapa nodded but didn't move until the four men climbed back into the Mercedes and closed the doors.

John looked at David who had been standing quietly by his side, his eyes cast down at his feet.

"Please join me in the back, Mr. Hayes. My son will sit in front."

John looked at David. David nodded unhappily and opened the front door. John bent down and sat beside Ronald Yu, closing the door behind him. Ronald tapped the driver's headrest with his cane, and the Rolls Royce glided away from the curb.

The seats were soft and well worn, the interior smelling of leather and a faint aroma of Tiger Balm. John sat quietly, not wanting to be the first to start the conversation. He had no idea what Ronald Yu's involvement was and was still trying to work out how all the pieces of the puzzle were supposed to fit together.

Apparently, David Yu wasn't sending threatening messages, but his father's men had beaten John up. Peter Croft was not the nice guy he made out to be, and the policeman, Joseph Wong had hit him on the back of his head and tied him up. It was all very puzzling. Who were the bad guys, and what was going on? Was everyone a bad guy?

In the corner of his eye, John could see Ronald Yu studying him. He was an elegant looking man, his hair grey and slicked back, his frame slim. John turned to look at him. His face was stern but not unkind, and his eyes sparkled with a keen intellect as he looked back at John.

"Well, Mr. Hayes, you have had a very busy week. Perhaps we should start from the beginning?"

"Perhaps you can start with why your men have been following me, and why they beat me up the other day."

"A fair question," Ronald Yu nodded. He glanced toward

his son sitting in the front seat. "Do you have children, Mr. Hayes?"

John shook his head.

"No? Well, Mr. Hayes, a father always wants the best for his children. I had a very tough life, it was a struggle, but as you can see," he waved his hand around the car interior, "fate has been very kind to me." His eyes flicked toward David again.

"I never wanted my son to struggle like I did. I gave him everything—the best education money can buy, a generous allowance, and helped fund his business ventures—but sometimes," Ronald sighed, "your children don't fulfill your expectations."

John glanced at David in the front whose shoulders had slumped, his head hanging as he looked down at his feet.

"I love my son, Mr. Hayes, but he is a disappointment. He has no business acumen, I constantly have to bail him out, and..." Ronald raised his voice and directed it toward the front seat, "he has a nasty gambling habit."

"I don't see what any of this has to do with me."

"No. Forgive me, Mr. Hayes. Let me explain. My son has borrowed money from a very nasty individual and hasn't paid it back."

David turned his head to look back. "You know?"

Ronald Yu muttered something in Cantonese, and David flinched and looked away.

"I will have to clean up his mess, Mr. Hayes, as I have done many times before. He is a disappointment, but he is my son, and I will never let any harm come to him. So, my men watch him around the clock, and when we saw you following him, we had you followed. I apologize for the beating... Sometimes, my men enjoy their job too much. I assumed someone had employed you to retrieve the money. Apparently, I was wrong."

John nodded, thinking over what he had said and how it explained certain events.

"Which brings us to today, Mr. Hayes. My son tells me you have saved his life, and for that, I am indebted. Perhaps you can explain what has been going on and let us see how we can resolve the matter."

John pursed his lips, considering his options. He needed help, and he didn't understand what was happening. Perhaps this old man could help him. He took a deep breath and exhaled slowly. Making his choice he started from the beginning, Ronald Yu listening carefully, only interrupting now and then for clarification. When John got to the part where he had left Joseph Wong tied up on the boat, Ronald chuckled.

"Mr. Hayes, assaulting a police officer? You are a very naughty man."

John shrugged. "I will worry about that later."

"Leave Inspector Wong to me. I know him. He is not a good man, and he is a terrible policeman. He has been a thorn in my side for a long time. I will take care of him." Ronald issued some instructions in Cantonese to his driver, who dialed a number on the phone attached to the dashboard and spoke. A moment later, the black G-Wagen in front of them peeled off and made a U-turn.

John studied Ronald for a moment. "Are you a Triad leader? *Sun Yee On*?"

David's shoulders tensed, but he said nothing. Ronald studied John for a moment, his face expressionless, then broke into a smile.

"Mr. Hayes, you must be careful making accusations like that in a city like this." He paused and gazed out through the windscreen. "In this city, things are not always what they at first seem. Peter Croft for example. A respectable business-man. A pillar of society. A regular contributor to charities. Am I right?"

John nodded, not sure where the conversation was going.

"Peter Croft is also not what he appears. His image is carefully cultivated, to all intents and purposes he can do no wrong. But Peter Croft has a dark side few are aware of." He smiled. "We all have a dark side, Mr. Hayes, but Peter's is darker than most."

"What do you mean?" John couldn't relate what Ronald was telling him with the Peter he had met although after being tied up on his boat, he had his suspicions.

"Peter's rags to riches story makes great reading. His parents were comfortably off but not rich. Yet now, Peter has great wealth."

"I've read his background. He is supposed to be a very astute property investor and developer."

Ronald smiled. "Yes, so it would appear." He looked over at David before continuing. "One thing a property investor is always short of is cash flow. He has large amounts of capital tied up for years in the hope of a future windfall profit. Sometimes, it's hard to fund a lifestyle and meet interest payments. It's something all developers struggle with. However, it doesn't seem to bother Peter." Ronald paused and studied John for a moment. "Do you know why?"

John shrugged. He had no idea, but he was sure he was about to find out.

"Peter Croft has... How do you say it? His fingers in many pies. Have you seen the recent news reports about record seizures of a drug called GBL?"

David turned and looked back over the seat, a puzzled expression on his face. "What do you mean, Father?"

Ronald waved his hand in irritation, instead waiting for John's answer.

"Yes, the date rape drug." John shook his head in disbelief. "No, you're not telling me he's involved?"

"Yes, Mr. Hayes. Peter is a major smuggler of GBL, Gamma-Butyrolactone. It's not just as you say, the date rape drug. It is also popular for its psychoactive properties. It's readily available in the bars of Lan Kwai Fong and Wan Chai."

"I can't believe it."

David looked stunned.

"It's true," replied Ronald. "He imports it from Lithuania. It's legal there and used as, believe it or not, a floor cleaner." He scowled at David. "Unfortunately, my son doesn't pay enough attention to his businesses or the people he does business with."

John looked from David to Ronald and back again. He just couldn't picture the man he had spent time with, the charming, successful businessman, as a drug peddler.

"Okay, let's say what you're telling me is true. What does it have to do with the threats I've received? I still can't see the connection. Does a competitor want him dead?"

David had now turned fully in his seat to face backward. He looked at his father who was sitting back in his seat, studying John closely.

"Mr. Hayes, let's again look at what we do know. Peter's side business has been suffering this year. There have been record seizures of GBL by Hong Kong customs. This month, two million dollars' worth of the drug was found in a flat in Central. Last month, they found another shipment in a parcel center. This is all affecting Peter's cash flow at a time when he needs it the most. He is bidding on a large site in the Central waterfront reclamation and has a lot of money flowing out with nothing flowing back. He is hurting."

"I still don't see how this is connected."

"I don't either, Mr. Hayes, but someone is trying to make it look like David is behind this. Who stands to gain if David is arrested?"

"I don't know."

"Think harder Mr. Hayes."

"You're telling me if David is arrested, Peter stands to benefit?"

"Yes."

"How?"

"I would imagine Peter would have David removed from the board and would take over his shareholding, giving him complete control of the company."

"But that's what Peter told me David planned by having him killed."

"Ha. You are being framed, Mr. Hayes. You are an unfortunate pawn in a larger game of chess."

John sat back in the seat, staring blankly at the headrest of the seat in front of him. He thought back over the events of the recent week, trying to make sense of what Ronald had told him, piecing it together with actual events.

"In the bar, when David was there," John spoke aloud, verbalizing his thoughts, "David got an anonymous call, telling him a *gweilo* was going to kill him. At that time, Peter was in the toilet. Then just after Peter left the bar, I received a text." John nodded to himself. "Yes, Peter was never in the same room with me when the texts were sent. Even later, when I was at his house, I received a text when he was in another room."

Ronald said nothing, just listening and nodding. David still faced backward, watching both of them.

"He could easily have planted the deposit slips in David's office for me to find."

"I told you I haven't been in that office all week," David piped up eagerly.

"Okay, here's a question for you. If what you say is true, why me? Why not use a professional assassin? If he is as crooked as you say, I'm sure he would have access to a hitman."

No-one answered. David turned and slumped back in his seat, facing the front while Ronald pulled back the window curtain and gazed out the side window at the buildings passing by.

After a few minutes, Ronald spoke, as if to himself, his eyes still focused on the buildings outside.

"Perhaps he didn't actually want you to succeed. He didn't want you to kill him. He just wanted to discredit my son. Frame him for attempted murder. That would still help him achieve his goal."

"But I would be a witness. I could say they forced me into it."

Ronald turned to face John. "You would be dead, Mr. Hayes. Killed by Inspector Joseph Wong as you tried to take Peter Croft's life."

"Fuck."

"Yes, Mr. Hayes. Fuck."

"But this still doesn't explain how he knew my name, my bank account, my phone number?"

"Hmmm. I've been thinking about that. Who in your life would have that information? Are you married?"

John shook his head, the memory of Charlotte like an icy blade piercing his heart.

"Not anymore."

"I'm sorry, Mr. Hayes."

Ronald paused for a moment, deep in thought.

"It could be someone in your office or someone at the bank. My thought is he bribed someone at the bank. They have all the information he would need."

"But why me?"

"That I don't know, Mr. Hayes."

38

The Rolls Royce had been climbing for a while, its 6.2-liter V8 engine having no trouble with the steep, winding roads that led up The Peak. John had been too involved in the conversation to pay attention to where they were going and was surprised to see the car pull up in front of a pair of elaborate wrought-iron gates. The gates slowly glided open, and the Rolls Royce slipped inside, turning around the fountain that took up the center of the turning circle before stopping in front of an old colonial-style mansion. The driver climbed out and opened Ronald's door.

"Come inside, Mr. Hayes, join me for some tea."

John nodded and watched as, with the help of his dragon-headed cane and the assistance of his driver, Ronald climbed out of the car.

John and David got out and waited for Ronald to make his way slowly around the car toward the front door of the house. Ronald was a small man, perhaps a head shorter than John, but despite his need for a cane, he held himself straight and with dignity.

The large, polished wood door opened, a housemaid in a black dress and a frilly white apron standing on the top step, waiting for Ronald to approach. She took him by the arm and walked with him inside, John and David following.

They walked through a large entrance hall with double-height ceilings and a black and white tile floor into a wide drawing room with French windows that opened out onto a garden filled with sculpted trees and bonsai.

The housemaid helped settle Ronald into an ornately carved wooden chair with a high back while John and David sat on a sofa opposite him.

"Will you have tea, Mr. Hayes, or..." Ronald's eyes twinkled, "would you prefer something a little stronger?"

John would have loved to have something stronger, but he needed to keep his wits about him.

"Please call me John, and tea will be fine, thank you."

Ronald looked at his son, "David..."

David stood up and disappeared out a side door.

John looked around while they waited for the tea to arrive. Fine silk carpets from China covered the parquet floors, and the carved rosewood furniture, although a bit heavy for John's taste, was obviously old and expensive. On the walls were Chinese watercolors of mountains covered in mist and panels of calligraphy.

David reappeared with another housemaid carrying a tray which she laid on the coffee table in front of Ronald. She started to serve, but Ronald waved her away as David quietly resumed his seat beside John.

"Do you like Chinese tea, John? It's quite different from your English tea. There are a lot more subtleties of flavor." John nodded politely as Ronald continued. "My favorite is *Ti Kuan Yin*. It comes from Fujian province in China." Ronald slid forward in his seat, picked up a jug of hot water and poured a little into a terracotta teapot. He swirled it around, warming the teapot, then poured the water out into a bowl. From a small porcelain jar, he took a spoonful of rolled tea leaves and added them to the teapot before filling it with hot water from the jug. He looked up at John and smiled.

"There is an interesting legend about how the tea gained its name. Have you heard of *Kuan Yin*, John?"

"Isn't she the Lady Buddha? The Buddha of Compassion?"

Ronald smiled. "You are correct, John."

"I first came across her in India. There they call her *Avalokiteshvara*."

"Are you a Buddhist, John?"

John frowned. "I no longer believe in God, Mr. Yu."

Ronald raised his eyebrows. "That is interesting, John. Why is that?"

"Let's just say things have happened that make me doubt the presence of an all-seeing, benevolent being. I believe we make our own destiny, and if something happens, we have to deal with it ourselves. There is little point in sitting back and hoping some divine presence will take care of things."

Ronald nodded gently, his keen eyes studying John's face. "You are an interesting man, John." He leaned forward and poured tea into three tiny porcelain cups. He held one out to John, then picked one up for himself, ignoring David who had to pick up his own. Ronald raised the cup and waited for John to take a sip before drinking his own. He licked his lips and set the cup down.

"Ahhh. My father used to serve this tea in our home back in China. It always brings back memories." He smiled at John.

"Perhaps you are right about God, John. But sometimes,

the stories of divinity make you feel happy and give you hope. This tea, for example. My father used to tell me the legend of a poor farmer who used to walk past a broken-down temple every day. In that temple was an iron statue of *Kuan Yin*. The poor farmer wanted to repair the temple but had no money to do so. So instead, one day, he swept it clean and lit some incense for the goddess.

"That night, he had a dream where *Kuan Yin* visited him and showed him a cave with a treasure he must share with others. The next day, he found the cave with a bush growing inside. He replanted the bush and shared cuttings with his neighbors. From this bush came the tea he named *Ti Kuan Yin* or Iron Buddha of Compassion." Ronald chuckled. "Who knows if it is true, but it's a nice little story for me to tell when I am drinking tea."

John smiled, and they sat in silence, sipping the hot flowery liquid. At that moment, there was a buzzing from Ronald's suit jacket pocket, and he reached inside and pulled out his phone. He squinted at the screen, then tapped it with his thumb and put it to his ear.

"*Wai,* Hello."

He listened carefully, nodding occasionally before issuing instructions in Cantonese and hanging up. He slid the phone back into his pocket, his face hard, the jovial grandfather expression nowhere in sight as he stared out the French windows into the garden. Eventually, he brought his gaze back to the room and turned to John.

"Our friend, Inspector Joseph Wong has been very co-operative. He has agreed to help us with our inquiries. I think we should see what he has to say." He picked up his cane from the side of his chair and with difficulty pushed himself to his feet. John and David placed their teacups on the table and stood.

Ronald glanced at his son, "Stay here."

"But Father."

"*Sau seng*, Be quiet!"

David's jaw clamped shut, and he stared unhappily at his feet. John raised an eyebrow but remained silent. He looked across at David. He felt sorry for him. He would never grow out of his father's considerable shadow, and in his father's eyes could never do anything right. No wonder he sought solace in the gambling tables.

He followed Ronald out the door to the waiting Rolls Royce.

39

They drove in silence for about twenty minutes, deep in their own thoughts. The car wound down from The Peak and crossed over to the southside of the island. Eventually, they reached the industrial area of Wong Chuk Hang, an area filled with drab and grimy buildings, eight to ten stories high, filled with multi-story warehousing and factories. The Rolls Royce pulled into one such building, turning into the wide entranceway, then followed the entrance ramp as it wound its way past loading docks and up to the higher levels of the building. At the top, John spotted the black G-Wagen parked beside a loading bay and one of Ronald's men standing, smoking a cigarette.

The Rolls Royce pulled up beside him, and John opened his door and got out. The black-clad thug scowled at John and threw his cigarette on the ground, not bothering to stub it out. He walked around to Ronald's side of the car, and in a manner completely at odds with his appearance, gently helped him out and led him by the arm up the steps beside the loading bay and through the battered wood double doors. John followed them through, then down a wide corridor, the walls scarred with damage from the passage of goods. A fluorescent light flickered overhead, and the air smelled of dust and stale urine.

The thug pushed open a door and guided Ronald inside. John followed him into a large, dimly lit warehouse space, empty apart from a chair in the center of the room. Joseph sat with his arms bound behind him, his legs fastened to the chair with plastic cable ties. His eyes were swollen shut, only slits, and his head was slumped to one side. Blood trickled from his left nostril, and his lips were split. Three of Ronald's men stood guard around him, all of them stiffening and straightening up as Ronald walked in.

One of the men rushed to the side of the warehouse and retrieved a chair which he placed in front of Joseph, and Ronald sat down. John stood beside him and stared at the battered form in front of him. Joseph didn't seem to be aware they had walked in, his lips moving as if he was talking to himself, his chest was moving up and down as he took rapid breaths. Ronald nodded at the man who had brought him in, and he stepped toward Joseph, opened a plastic bottle of water, and tipped the contents over his head.

Joseph lifted his head and looked around, noticing Ronald and John for the first time. He cleared his throat and spat a globule of saliva and blood onto the floor. He sniffed and straightened his head, looking first at John, then fixed his eyes on Ronald. John thought he detected a trace of fear as he looked at Ronald.

Ronald studied him for a moment. "Inspector Wong, we meet again. Let's stick to English so Mr. Hayes can understand."

Joseph sniffed again and spat on the floor. He looked at

John and sneered. He appeared to be missing a few teeth. "*Tiu leh lo moh.* Motherfucker."

One of Ronald's men stepped forward, and John winced as the man punched Joseph on the side of the head, knocking him to the floor.

The man bent over, set the chair and Joseph upright again, and stepped back.

Ronald leaned forward, his hands resting on the cane planted on the floor between his legs. He narrowed his eyes, his voice filled with steel.

"I suggest you show us a little more respect, Inspector Wong."

"Okay, okay."

"Why don't you start from the beginning?"

Joseph raised his head, regarded Ronald for a moment, then his shoulders sagged, any last vestiges of defiance leaving his body.

He started slowly, his voice a mumble, and John had to strain to hear what he was saying.

"It was Peter's idea... His drug shipments have been hit hard in recent months... His cash-flow is tight." He paused for breath, and when he resumed, his voice was louder. "When he found out about David's gambling debts, he decided we would frame David, get him thrown in prison so he could take over the company and divert the company funds."

John spoke up. "But why me?"

Joseph laughed. At least John thought he laughed. It was more like a grunt followed by a cough and a sob.

"Why you?... Why you?... You were just some random customer at the bank. We bribed someone at the bank to find us someone who needed money, whose account was in debt. They picked you... stupid fuckers." He looked up at

John. "Why couldn't you have just gone along with it?" He shook his head, and his chin dropped to his chest, the effort of talking taxing his body.

"Who was texting me?"

Joseph sighed. "That was Peter... The bank guy gave us your number. We got a burner SIM, and Peter sent you the texts."

John watched him for a moment, the pieces of the puzzle slowly falling into place. It was all starting to make sense.

"Where is Peter now?"

Joseph looked up. "How the fuck would I know? The bastard left me when those Nepali fuckers attacked me."

John looked at Ronald who was still leaning forward on his cane, frowning at Joseph.

Ronald spoke up, his voice quiet but firm. "I want you to give my men a list of all your contacts, all your dealers, all your corrupt colleagues on the force."

"No way... I'll be finished."

Ronald glanced at the man standing to Joseph's left, and he stepped forward. He held a two-foot length of bamboo in his hand. He raised it high above his head with both hands before bringing it down hard with a resounding crack on Joseph's left thigh. Joseph screamed in pain, and the man stepped back to his previous position. Joseph's screams turned to sobs, his whole body shuddering.

Ronald watched him, his face devoid of expression as the sobs subsided to whimpers. Joseph looked up at Ronald and pleaded.

"They will kill me. I have a wife, a daughter."

"Then I suggest you cooperate, Inspector Wong. Only then can we help you." Ronald nodded at his man, and he stepped forward raising the bamboo pole above his head.

"Okay, okay," Joseph protested, trying to make himself smaller. The man stepped back, and Joseph's head dropped down again, his body shaking in silent sobs.

Ronald pushed himself to his feet and turned to John.

"I think we have heard enough." He nodded to his men, then turned toward the door. John followed him out, and just before he exited the door, he looked back at Joseph, slumped in the chair, surrounded by Ronald's men who stared back at him, their faces blank and expressionless. John didn't like the guy, but seeing a fellow human being reduced to a bruised and bloody lump of flesh made him sick. He didn't see much promise in Inspector Joseph Wong's future. Still, Joseph would have killed him, so John supposed he deserved it. He steeled himself, turned and walked out.

He slid into the Rolls Royce beside Ronald, and the car glided away down the ramp to ground level. As it pulled out into daylight and accelerated gently up the road, John cleared his throat and asked the question he didn't actually want to know the answer to.

"What will happen to him?"

Ronald didn't answer immediately, just looked out the front window, his eyes focused on something far away. John thought he hadn't heard him and was about to ask again when Ronald answered.

"He threatened my family, John. No one does that." He turned to look at John. "You need not worry about him anymore. Let's just say, he will be providing one of our new buildings a lot of support at ground level."

John swallowed, closed his eyes, and tried to think of something else.

40

J ohn was tired and fed up. He cricked his head left to right and rolled his shoulders, first forward, then back, leaning back in the leather seat of the black Toyota Alphard. Two of Ronald's men sat in the front, Tejpal sat next to him in the middle row, and Thapa reclined in the back. They had been there on the side of the road for two hours, and John just wanted to get out. One of the men in the front kept farting, and the air in the car was stale, rank, and stuffy.

John had been faced with a choice. Walk away from the situation with the money in his account and the knowledge he wouldn't be troubled by Joseph Wong anymore or find Peter and get some form of closure. He had been undecided, and Ronald had left the choice up to him. It was only when he had accessed the voice recordings stored in the cloud from the listening device he had planted in the saloon on the Pegasus, that his mind was made up.

With Ronald, he had listened to them in the car on the way back from the warehouse, and the evidence had been damning. Once they had fast forwarded the lunch conversations between Peter and David, they heard Peter discussing with Joseph how they would kill John and place his body in the saloon in such a way, it would look like he had been killed attempting to murder Peter. When they discussed what to do with David, Ronald sat forward and listened intently, a small twitch in the corner of his mouth the only clue as to his anger. Peter and Joseph had finally decided to kill David too and dispose of his body at sea while making sure all evidence pointed to his involvement in the attempted murder of Peter. After all, a dead man can't deny the evidence stacked against him.

Ronald sat back in his seat and regarded John with an intensity he hadn't experienced before.

"John, it is up to you what you decide to do from here onward, but I will not rest until this man is brought to justice for what he has tried to do."

John nodded. He didn't reply immediately and watched the world pass by the window of the Rolls Royce. He didn't want to ask what "justice" Ronald had in mind, but he too wanted closure. He turned back to Ronald.

"I'm in."

Ronald's men had been watching Peter's house all evening, but there had been no sign of the man. Another man was on the boat and another outside Peter's office. Ronald had more men at the airport at Chek Lap Kok, but Peter was nowhere to be seen. They assumed he would come home at some stage. Even if he was planning to flee the country, he would need cash and his passport. John had the keys to the house, but there were two problems. Imelda and the other housemaid were in the house, and John assumed there would be an alarm for which he didn't know the code. Ronald didn't have a solution either but offered his men as manpower. All John could do was wait and pounce when an opportunity presented itself. He closed his eyes and tried to rest. The strain of the previous week had been exhausting, and he just wanted to go somewhere quiet and sleep for days.

He thought back to the last time he had been sitting in a car waiting, back in India, when he had hunted down the men who had harmed his wife. Even now, the thought stirred anger in his stomach. Anger and a rekindling of the grief he always felt when he remembered Charlotte. She had meant everything to him, and his life would never be the same now she was gone. What had he done to deserve a life like this? He had come to Hong Kong to escape the stress and bad memories, only for bad luck to follow him and throw him into a life and death situation where his moral compass was tested once again.

At around nine p.m., the men in front stiffened, and the driver reached back and nudged John. The gate at Peter's house was sliding open.

"Thapa, Mr. Rai," John whispered and felt them stir. Five pairs of eyes stared at the main gate, watching to see who would emerge. Imelda and the other Filipina, whose name John had never learned, stepped out and headed down the road toward the bus stop as the gate slid shut behind them. Sunday was the traditional day off for domestic staff, most of them gathering in their thousands in the streets of Central, and Imelda and her colleague were obviously going to make the most of it, leaving home the night before.

The men relaxed and settled back down again to wait. Once the house staff had been gone for an hour, and the street was dark and quiet, they decided to move. They were all dressed in black, but just before they opened the doors, Tejpal turned to John.

"You will need some of this. It's left over from my army

days. I knew it would come in useful." He dipped his fingers into a small plastic container of black cream and smeared it liberally on John's face. "It's a full moon tonight, and your pale skin will show up in the moonlight." He made sure it covered John's neck and the backs of his hands before sitting back and examining his handiwork. "Good."

"What about you and Thapa?"

"Look at our color," Tejpal laughed. "We have natural camouflage."

Ronald's men looked back and grinned, the first time John had seen them smile.

John, Thapa, and Tejpal slid open the side door and climbed out, leaving Ronald's men inside the Alphard to watch the street. They looked both ways, then jogged across the road and headed toward Peter's house. They spied a section of the boundary wall that abutted a large banyan tree, its branches spreading wide over the road and over the wall into Peter's property. John boosted Thapa up the trunk, who then climbed until he reached a branch that spread out over Peter's compound. Thapa made himself secure and reached down to pull up Tejpal. Both then reached down and hoisted John up into the branches from where they dropped down into the garden at the rear of the triple garage. The three men crouched and listened for a moment, but the house was silent. The muffled sound of a passing car carried from the road outside, and from deep inside the storm-water drain, a couple of bullfrogs croaked, their booming calls amplified in the confined space.

The three men spread out, Thapa to the corner of the garage where he could observe the gate, and Tejpal headed down the slope and underneath the cantilevered pool deck where he settled into the undergrowth. From there he could watch for any approach from the lower part of the hillside. It would be unlikely as the slope was precipitously steep, but they needed to cover all angles of approach, and Tejpal needed to use all his mountaineering skills gleaned from a childhood in Nepal to avoid slipping and falling below. John skirted close to the house, crouching low to stay below the windows and slid up next to the front entrance. He peered into the darkened interior through the glass panel at the side of the door. Ronald's men had been watching the house all day, so they were confident now the maids had left, there was no-one else at home. The telltale blinking of a red LED on a control panel on the entrance wall gave away the presence of an alarm, so John would have to use Plan B. He had the set of keys he had taken from Peter's jacket on the boat in his pocket but with the alarm on didn't want to risk unlocking the door. He would wait. In a crouching run, he dashed across to the far side of the compound and crawled inside a bed of canna lilies, wedging himself against the boundary wall where he could remain unobserved but keep an eye on the front door as well as the side door which opened into the kitchen. He settled down to wait, confident no-one would spot them in their dark clothing.

The time went slowly, John glad of the fact it wasn't raining but wished the temperature was a bit cooler. Even at night, the humidity levels were high, and amongst the garden foliage, there was no breeze to move the air around. His clothes clung to his body and sweat mingled with the cam cream and ran into his eyes. He wiped his eyes with his shirt sleeve, taking care to move slowly. He wondered how the other two were coping. He didn't need to worry about Tejpal, he had a lot of experience patrolling the border between Hong Kong and China before the 1997 handover.

But Thapa had been raised in the city with little experience of waiting quietly in the undergrowth for an enemy to appear. However, John was confident in the resilience of his Nepali friends. They had an inherent toughness, and he was sure they would cope with whatever came his way.

John stole a look at his G-Shock. He had been there for two hours, but there was still no sign of Peter. He had to return to the house at some stage—the question was when. Another hour passed, and John was giving up hope. There was only so much time he could sit in a tropical garden. He hoped there were no snakes, and so far, there had been only cockroaches roaming through the undergrowth and crawling across his feet. He had given up fighting off the mosquitoes, allowing them to suck freely on his exposed skin. He wished he had remembered mosquito repellent when they were making their plan.

He felt the telltale buzz of his cell phone vibrating in his pocket. He reached in and pulled it out, shielding the phone with his shirt so the glow of the screen couldn't be seen. *"He's come."* John had set up a WhatsApp group for all the watchers so they could receive the message at the same time. He stiffened and peered through the foliage as the front gate slid open. A dark shape slipped inside and paused by the wall, waiting for the gate to slide shut again. John couldn't make out his face yet and waited until the figure crossed the parking area and headed toward the front door. It was Peter. John typed a message and pressed send.

"I see him. Leave him to me. Wait for my message."

He watched as Peter unlocked the front door and stepped inside. John saw him pause by the alarm control panel, then close the door behind him. Time for John to move. He slowly rose to his feet and pushed his way through the foliage until he was out of the garden and crouching on the driveway. He crawled across to the wall of the house where he wouldn't be observed from inside and stood up. He shook the stiffness out of his legs and rolled his shoulders. He seemed to spend too much of his life hiding in wait for people.

He looked across to the garage and spotted Thapa crouched by the corner of the garage, watching him. He gave him a thumbs up and saw the white of Thapa's teeth as he grinned.

John took a deep breath, then crept toward the front door, glancing inside through the glass side panel. Peter couldn't be seen, but the LED on the alarm was now blinking green. John peered at the door lock, then removed the keys from his pocket, selected the key most likely to fit, and unlocked the door.

41

J ohn slipped inside and pushed the door closed softly behind him. He paused for a moment, listening to the sounds of the house. It was silent, but as he listened, he heard the muffled sound of someone moving around inside. John reached behind him and pulled the Glock from his waistband and held it out in front of him—he hoped he wouldn't have to use it. Slowly, very slowly, he stepped forward, grateful for the marble floors—no creaking floorboards to give him away. He remembered the layout of the house from his previous visit, and the moonlight coming in through the full-height windows provided enough light for him to find his way around. He crept forward, through the entrance hall. To the right, he remembered a door opened onto a study. Moving toward it, he paused with his ear close to the door. There was no sound from inside, so with his left hand, he gently eased the door handle down and opened it. The room was dark inside, obviously no-one there. He closed the door again and turned to his left. He crept forward and peered through the doorway into the large living room. He scanned it quickly, but again, there was no-one there. Keeping close to the rear wall of the living room, away from the windows, he moved swiftly toward the dining room and peered inside. Empty. He tried the kitchen next. The recessed lights under the overhead cupboards were on, providing a soft glow and a quick look sufficed to show there was no one inside. John heard more noise. Peter was downstairs. As if to confirm this, John's phone buzzed again. With his left hand, he removed it from his pocket to view the message from Tejpal.

"I can see him moving around in the bedroom. He's packing an overnight bag."

John thought quickly. The top floor was the only way out of the building. He would wait for him up here. He crept back into the living room and looked around. Selecting an armchair in a darkened rear corner, out of immediate sight of the stairway, John sat down to wait.

He placed the Glock on his lap and thought about what to do next. He had an idea. From his other pocket, he removed the phone he had found in Peter's jacket on the boat. The phone was locked, but John had studied it closely, and the screen, viewed from an angle, showed a pattern of fingerprints. It had taken eight attempts and almost an hour —the phone locking him out for a period after several failed attempts—before he had miraculously unlocked the phone. Once he was in, he changed the pin code and on impulse, went to the messaging app history. There was only one number—his. He opened the messages and found the final proof he had been looking for. A complete record of the texts that were sent from this phone to his. It was the final nail in Peter's coffin. Whether that expression remained a metaphor, John hadn't decided.

After five minutes, he heard someone climbing the

stairs. He stiffened, picked up the Glock, and readied himself. Peter hurried into the living room, carrying an overnight bag in his left hand and a pouch in his right. John waited until he was halfway through the living room on his way to the front door, then pressed send on the phone.

Immediately, an alert sounded from Peter's pocket. He stopped, set the bag down and pulled his phone out of his pocket. He looked at the screen and swore. Despite himself, John grinned. He knew what the screen said. Peter had just received a text from a hidden number.

"Going somewhere?"

"Turn around." John flicked on the lamp beside his chair and stood up as Peter whirled around, a look of shock on his face. He raised his hands and backed away as he caught sight of John pointing the Glock at him.

"Stay where you are, Peter, this one is actually loaded."

"John? Is that you? What's that on your face?"

Peter tried a smile, but his eyes darted around the room, looking for a way out, an avenue of escape.

"Don't even think about it, Peter. I've used one of these before, and I won't hesitate to use it again." He gestured with the Glock toward an armchair. "Sit down over there."

Peter moved to the armchair and sat down, his initial shock replaced with an expression of calculation—his business mind already computing the risk/reward ratios and looking for an exit strategy.

"I can explain everything, John. Please put the gun down."

"Yes, why don't you, Peter. And you can forget about me putting the gun down. It's staying pointed at your head."

Peter sighed. "I can pay you, John. I'm rich. I'll give you whatever you want."

"Really?" John moved closer and perched his butt on the

arm of the sofa. "From what I hear, you are no longer as rich as you say you are."

"Ha," Peter scoffed. "Look around you. Do I look poor to you?"

"G.B.L."

"What?" Peter's arrogant expression slipped.

"You know what I mean, Peter. G.B.L. As in gamma-Butyrolactone."

"I don't know what you are talking about," Peter blustered, his arrogance now gone.

"Don't lie, Peter. I have a gun pointed at your head. I know what you've been up to. You've spread the company's finances too thin. You're struggling to make payments, and on top of that, your wife is leaving you. That will be expensive." John paused, studying Peter's face for a reaction, but he wasn't giving much away.

"I know you started importing G.B.L to keep the company and yourself in cash flow. I also know you've had your last few shipments seized. So you panicked. You heard about David's gambling debts, so you came up with a plan to frame him and take over his share of the company. You and your friend Inspector Wong. Am I right?"

Peter shook his head. "Rubbish," he scoffed. "You don't know what you're talking about. I am an honest businessman, and Inspector Wong, when he gets hold of you, will ensure you are locked up for a very long time."

John smiled. "I don't think Inspector Wong will be making use of this planet's resources anymore."

"What do you mean?" Peter's facial expression changed as realization slowly dawned on him. His jaw dropped open. "You killed him? A police officer?"

"From what I hear, Peter, your friend Joseph was a

disgrace to the uniform he wore. I don't think the Hong Kong Police Force will miss him."

Peter finally slumped in his chair, all trace of the confident wheeler-dealer gone. He stared at the floor for a while before looking up at John

"So, you have it all figured out?"

"Most of it Peter. But one thing I do want to ask. Why me?"

Peter didn't answer for a while as if he hadn't heard the question. When he spoke, it wasn't much more than a whisper, and John had to strain to hear him.

"It was Joseph's idea. We bribed someone at the bank for your personal records."

"But why me?"

Peter looked up slowly. "You were just a random person with an overdraft. We didn't choose you. The bank staff gave us a file. It just happened to be you."

John looked away and breathed a sigh of relief. His secret was still safe. This had nothing to do with Bangalore. He looked back at the man whose greed had been the cause of a week of fear and confusion.

"So you thought you could screw up my life? Just like that?"

Peter shrugged. He had no answer.

"Why didn't you sell the boat? Your cars?"

"You don't understand, John," Peter shook his head. "If I did that, my competitors, the banks, my suppliers... they would all swoop in like vultures. It would finish me."

John stood up and paced around the room, Peter's eyes following him.

"What are you going to do? Call the police?"

John paused and turned back to face Peter. He narrowed his eyes and thought for a moment.

"Well, here's the thing, Peter. I've suddenly got a million dollars in my account, and I like the feeling of that. If I involve the police, I'll have to give the money back. It's evidence."

Peter's face lit up, seeing a way out.

"John, I'll double it. I'll give you whatever you want. Take one of the Porsches."

John walked back over to stand in front of Peter, waving the Glock at him.

"I don't think, Peter, you are in any position to be making any offers right now. I don't believe anything you say anymore, and besides, I'm sure you've already borrowed against all your assets. I doubt you truly own anything outright."

"No, John, I mean it. Look in the bag. There's cash in there. Take it. Keep it. Just let me go. I will never bother you again."

"Is that right?"

John's phone buzzed in his pocket, he removed it with his left hand, and glanced at the screen. He slipped it back into his pocket and grinned at Peter.

"Anyway, it's not me you have to worry about now."

"What do you mean?" Peter looked puzzled.

His eyes darted toward the door as the black-clad Thapa and Tejpal walked in and stood beside John. Peter looked at them both, then back at John.

"I'll give money to them, too." He looked first at Thapa, then Tejpal. "How much do you want?" Neither man spoke as Tejpal slid the Khukuri from the leather sheath fastened to his waist, the blade gleaming in the lamplight. Peter's eyes widened in panic.

"I'll give you anything you want."

"I told you, it's not us you need to worry about."

Peter looked back and forth between the three in confusion.

"Then who?"

A movement at the door caught his eye. Ronald's two men from the Alphard walked in and padded softly toward them, silent as cats.

"Who are they?" Peter's eyes flicked from them to John and back again as he watched them line up in front of him and cross their tattooed arms on their chests, their faces hard and expressionless.

John smiled. "Wait and see."

They all heard movement, and John watched Peter's face as his eyes darted toward the door. For the first time, he saw real fear on Peter's face as he recognized the man walking in. John didn't turn, just waited as the sound of slow footsteps and the rhythmic tap of a cane drew nearer.

Peter's lip quivered, all signs of confidence and bluster having left him.

"Peter, I think you know Mr. Yu. Thapa, Mr. Rai, why don't we give these fine gentlemen some space so they can get reacquainted?"

John turned and smiled at Ronald. Ronald placed a hand on John's arm and nodded, then moved past him and slowly eased himself down on the sofa. John looked back at Peter, his face hard.

"This will teach you not to play with people's lives."

He handed the Glock to Ronald's man, turned and walked toward the door, Tejpal and Thapa following behind. John picked up the sports bag as he walked out. Just before he reached the door, he heard Peter cry out.

"Wait."

John looked back over his shoulder.

"Who are you, really?"

John turned and smiled. "I thought you knew that Peter. I'm John Hayes."

42

J ohn took a sip of his masala chai, then placed the steel cup onto the Formica-topped table in front of him. He looked at the men sitting opposite him and smiled.

"I want to thank you both for everything you have done. I couldn't have done it without you."

"What are friends for John?" Thapa grinned. "Besides, I think my father really enjoyed himself. Didn't you, Papa?"

"Civilian life can get a bit boring, John. I haven't had as much fun since I left the service," Tejpal chuckled.

A small plump lady approached the table with a plate of steaming mo-mos.

"John, I would like to introduce you to my mother." John pushed back his chair and stood, pressing his hands together in front of his chest.

"Namaste."

She smiled shyly, placed the plate on the table, then retreated quickly to the kitchen.

The cafe was empty, the normally bustling streets of Yau Ma Tei quiet at that time of night. John looked around the room at the pictures of the Himalayas on the walls and the small temple of Mahakali on the rear wall, smoke from the twin incense sticks spiraling lazily toward the ceiling. He felt a hollowness in the pit of his stomach, the surroundings reminding him too much of India and Charlotte. He snapped himself out of it and reached down for the bag at his feet, placing it on his lap and unzipping it.

Inside was a change of clothes, a passport and four bundles of US dollars. He stacked the bundles on the table as Tejpal and Thapa watched. Placing the bag back on the floor, John then pushed a bundle each in front of Tejpal and Thapa.

"I want you to have this."

Thapa protested, but John stopped him.

"I couldn't have done it without you. You saved my life."

Thapa looked at his father who nodded back at him.

"Thank you, John," Thapa grinned. "Let us know when we can help you again."

John laughed. "I hope I never have to ask you again! Now, let me try one of these mo-mos. I'm starving."

The three men sipped tea and finished the mo-mos in silence.

"Oh, wait." Thapa jumped up and went out the back. He returned with the bag from the boat, a big grin on his face, passing it over to John. "We forgot about this one."

"Well, why not," John smiled and added the cash from the bag to the piles on the table. "Now, do you have anything stronger than Chai?"

Thapa and his father grinned at each other.

"*Raksi!*" they both exclaimed.

The car was waiting as the message had said it would, the black Alphard from the stakeout on Saturday. John walked off the ferry with all the other Monday morning commuters and up the ramp to the road. The side door slid open as he approached, and he looked inside. It was empty apart from the driver, one of Ronald's tattooed enforcers, looking back from the front seat. John nodded a greeting, and the man nodded back, the corner of his mouth twitching as if he wanted to smile but wasn't sure if he should. He climbed in, made himself comfortable, and the door slid quietly closed behind him.

John had slept most of Sunday, but he was still tired, his nervous system taxed by the strain of the previous week. Staying up until three a.m., drinking *Raksi* with Thapa and his father, Tejpal, hadn't helped either, but they had needed to blow off steam and relax after Saturday's events.

He settled back in the seat and closed his eyes as the Alphard eased its way through the morning traffic. He assumed they were heading to Ronald's house on The Peak, but ten minutes later, when he realized they hadn't started climbing, he opened his eyes and saw they were passing the Happy Valley Racecourse and headed for the Aberdeen Tunnel, taking them underneath Mount Parker to the southern side of the Island. He shrugged and watched the scenery pass as he thought about what he should do next. With his share of the cash he had found in the bags and the million Hong Kong dollars already in his account, he had almost half a million U.S. dollars. He didn't need to work for a while, and indeed, he didn't want to go back to working in an office. The mind-numbing boredom of the previous year held no appeal. Once again, he would set off for new pastures and make a fresh start.

Once through the tunnel, the car headed past Ocean Park, then turned left, following the signs for the Aberdeen Marina. John smiled, he had an idea where they were heading. The Alphard pulled up outside the marina entrance, and the side door slid open, letting in a blast of hot air. The driver looked back and nodded, the corner of his mouth twitching again. John smiled.

"*M goi sai leh,* thank you very much."

The driver's eyebrows raised in surprise, and he nodded again, this time both sides of his mouth twitching. John seemed to be making progress.

He climbed out, the heat and humidity an immediate contrast to the chilled interior of the Alphard. He stretched his back and looked around. It was too early for the queues to start forming for the Jumbo Restaurant, and the street was quiet. The sky overhead was cloudless and blue, and in the trees lining the footpath, mynahs squawked and squabbled as they started their day. John stepped onto the dock and followed the path around the edge of the marina until he reached the pontoon for the larger motor yachts. He walked to the end and looked up at the sleek black hull of the Pegasus.

Had it only been two days ago he had been tied up in the cabin, his life in danger? How quickly things can change. He narrowed his eyes against the glare from the sun reflecting off the water and the surrounding white hulled yachts and looked closer at the boat. The tender was still missing, but a pile of shoes waited on the dock. He slipped off his own and climbed the short flight of steps onto the rear deck. As he approached the door to the saloon, it slid open, and one of Ronald's black-clad enforcers stepped out. He nodded at John, no trace of a smile, and with a jerk of his head, indicated John should step inside. John paused, studied the man's face for a moment, then stepped into the saloon. The door slid shut behind him, and he was immediately chilled by the air-conditioned interior, his sweat-soaked shirt sticking to his skin.

"John, welcome. Thank you for coming."

Ronald Yu sat at the dining table at the end of the saloon, David Yu standing nervously beside him.

"Good morning."

"Please, come and take a seat. Will you have some tea?"

"Yes, thank you." John pulled out a chair and sat down as a man John hadn't seen before, wearing a polo shirt with "Pegasus" embroidered on the left breast, placed a small porcelain cup in front of John and proceeded to fill it with tea.

John waited, then raised the cup to his lips and took a sip. It was earthy and dark. "Mmm, this one is different from the other day."

"Yes, John. This is *Pu-Errh*. A fermented tea from Yunnan in South West China. Good for digestion."

"I like it." He took another sip, set the cup down on the table, and looked at Ronald and David expectantly.

"Have you read the newspaper this morning, John?"

"No, I haven't."

Ronald looked up at David and nodded. David picked up a copy of the South China Morning Post from the galley countertop and slid it across the table in front of John.

John looked down at the newspaper and read the headline stretched across the front page.

Peter Croft, Chairman of Pegasus Land, found dead.

John raised an eyebrow, glanced up at Ronald, and went back to reading.

"Property developer and philanthropist, Peter Croft was found dead at his home on Sunday evening. His body was found at the foot of the slope beneath his pool deck by a domestic helper when she returned home to find the house unlocked and the doors to the pool deck open. Police are investigating, but a spokesman said all signs point to an apparent suicide. Mr. Croft's estranged wife, currently in Singapore, was not available for comment."

John sat back in his chair and regarded Ronald Yu, the elderly man's face giving nothing away.

"That is unfortunate. He didn't strike me as the suicidal type."

"No, but one never truly knows the inner workings of another's mind. I would imagine, John, the truth will come out in the next few days. The public will no doubt learn about his considerable personal debts and the stress he has been under with the collapse of his marriage."

John looked at David, "And your son?"

"My son, John, has promised to make a fresh start. Haven't you, son?" Ronald looked sternly up at David who nodded. "No more gambling for him, and besides, he has a property company to take care of. Now that Peter has sadly left us, my son will need to take a much more active role. Under my strict supervision, of course."

"Of course." John smiled at David, "You will do well."

David smiled back nervously. "Thank you, John."

A flicker of irritation passed across Ronald's face, but it disappeared as quickly as it had appeared.

"And you, John, what are your plans now? I could use a resourceful man like you in my organization."

John sighed, leaned back in his chair, and gazed out the window as a sampan chugged slowly past.

"That's a kind offer, Mr. Yu, but I am going to take a break. Maybe travel a bit. I need some peace and quiet in my life for a while. After that, who knows?"

Ronald nodded slowly.

"You saved my son's reputation and possibly his life, John. He has disappointed me in many ways, but he is family, and I will forever be indebted to you. My offer stands, and if you ever need anything in the future, you know where I am. The money in the sports bag probably won't keep you going for very long."

John looked up in surprise as Ronald looked back with a trace of amusement. He waved his hand.

"Keep it. You earned it."

"Thank you, Mr. Yu." John looked around the interior of the boat. "What will happen to this? Will you keep it?"

"I like to run a tight ship, John, if you will pardon the expression. This boat is an unnecessary expense. I will sell it and reinvest the money into the company."

Ronald reached into his jacket pocket and pulled out a silver card case. He removed a cream-colored business card and slid it across the table.

"Here are my numbers, John. Remember, I am just a phone call away."

John looked from Ronald to David and back again.

"Thank you both very much."

44

John waded to the edge of the pool, pulled himself out of the water, walking across to the sun lounger to pick up his towel. As he dried himself, he looked around at the other guests. Next to him, an overweight middle-aged couple turned red in the sun while their child played with a water pistol. Across the pool, a young lady in a red bikini tried to catch his attention with a smile, but he ignored her. He still wasn't ready. He toweled himself down and pulled on a shirt. His skin was deeply tanned, and daily runs and swims in the resort's pool had stripped away the excess fat. It had been three months since he left his life in Hong Kong and flown straight to Bangkok, but after a couple of days in the frenetic city, he craved somewhere quieter. He had worked his way along the coast—Pattaya, Hua Hin, and many lesser-known beach-side towns—before jumping on a boat to the island of Koh Samui where he spent the past couple of months. He loved the island. It was quieter than its better-known counterpart, Phuket on the west coast of Thailand and was just what he needed after the stress and strain of the events involving Peter Croft.

Eventually, though, he would need to find work. He was managing his funds carefully, but they wouldn't last forever.

Slipping on his flip-flops, he walked between the cabins to his room. As he passed the open-sided, thatched roof reception, he smiled and waved at Tony, the resort manager.

"*Sawasdee krup.*"

"*Sawasdee krup, Khun* John. I have a package for you. It came this morning."

John frowned. No-one knew he was here. He walked toward the reception desk and took the manila envelope. It was addressed to John Hayes, but had no indication where it had come from.

"Who delivered this?"

"I don't know, *Khun* John. It was here when I came on duty. Is there a problem?"

"No, no, it's okay," John smiled. "Thank you."

Turning, he walked through the tropical garden to his cabin and unlocked the door. He kicked off his flip-flops and walked inside, throwing his towel on the bed, then sat in the cane chair by the window. With his thumb, he slit open the flap of the envelope and looked inside at the folded papers. He pulled them out and opened them. A news clipping fell onto his lap, and he picked it up to examine it closely.

Taken from the South China Morning Post from two days previously, the headline read: *Pegasus Land reaches new heights in IPO.* John read further: Shares of Pegasus Land have soared to eighty dollars on the first day of trading on the Hong Kong Stock Exchange, a clear sign of the confidence the public has in new Chairman, Ronald Yu's leadership. After the tragic suicide of the previous Chairman, Peter Croft, rumors abounded of the company's dire financial condition, but under Ronald Yu, the company has pared back debts and already significantly increased cash flow.

Chief Executive Officer, David Yu, in an announcement to the Stock Exchange, expressed his confidence for the future of the company and their intention to bid on several Government redevelopment projects in the future. A market analyst for Sino Securities commented, on the condition of anonymity, "Everything Ronald Yu touches turns to gold, so we are very bullish on this company's shares."

John chuckled to himself. "Ronald Yu, you wily old bastard."

He folded the news clipping and turned his attention to the other pieces of paper. The top sheet held one line of text. *With the blessings of Kuan Yin.*

Puzzled, John turned it over and looked at the sheet of paper underneath. It was a share certificate issued in his name—a shareholding in Pegasus Land. John looked at the number of shares and did a quick calculation. Leaning back in his chair, he gazed out the window, the papers falling to his side. Based on the share price in the news article, he was now a wealthy man.

READY FOR THE NEXT ADVENTURE?

The next book is currently being written, but if you sign up for my VIP newsletter I will let you know as soon as the next book is released.

By signing up for the newsletter you will also receive a complimentary copy of **Vengeance,** the first book in the John Hayes series, as well as advance notice of all new-releases.

Your email will be kept 100% private and you can unsubscribe at any time.

If you are interested, please visit my website

www.markdavidabbott.com
(No Spam. Ever.)

ALSO BY MARK DAVID ABBOTT

Vengeance - John Hayes Book 1

When a loved one is taken from you, and the system lets you down, what would you do?

John Hayes' life is perfect. He has a dream job in an exotic land, his career path is on an upward trajectory and at home he has a beautiful wife whom he loves with all his heart.

But one horrible day a brutal incident tears this all away from him and his life is destroyed.

He doesn't know who is to blame, he doesn't know what to do, and the police fail to help.

What should he do? Accept things and move on with his life or take action and do what the authorities won't do for him?

What would you do?

Vengeance is the first novel in the John Hayes series.

Available now on Amazon

ACKNOWLEDGMENTS

I would like to thank the following without whose support this book wouldn't have been possible.

My wife K, for encouraging me to continue writing and who frequently dragged me out from the pit of self doubt. My editor Sandy Ebel - Personal Touch Editing whose advice and input has made me "rite proppa", Angie-O e-Covers for a rocking cover, and my Beta readers Sid and Ritz for always being helpful and encouraging.

Although I have spent a large portion of my life living in and visiting Hong Kong there were parts of the story where I needed the input of others. Christina Tang, without your help regarding the operation of Casinos, the first chapter would not have been possible.

Thank you Madhav Shankar for your advice regarding banking regulations, and thank you to Anil Daryanani, Thuan Forrester and Chau Kei Ngai for your help with Cantonese. Anil, your knowledge of Cantonese swear words is disturbingly encyclopaedic. A big thanks to Krish Gaurav for your help with Nepalese.

Anil D'Souza, thank you for your input on matters

nautical, and Paul Schwerdt, your answers to my military questions were invaluable.

Thank you to my Advanced Reader Team, particularly Kathryn Defranc, Frances Sim-Higgins, Thomas Webb, Manali Rohinesh, David Roche and Terje Olsen. It's your input that has helped make the book what it is.

But most of all, a big thanks to you, my readers. It is your support and feedback that make the task of writing a joyful experience.

ABOUT THE AUTHOR

Mark can be found online at:
    www.markdavidabbott.com

on Facebook
    www.facebook.com/markdavidabbottauthor

on Twitter
    twitter.com/abbott_author

on Instagram
    instagram.com/thekiwigypsy

or on email at:
    www.markdavidabbott.com/contact

Printed in Great Britain
by Amazon